GOD, WHEN WILL I EVER BELONG?

"God, when will I ever belong?"

Written by Katherine D. Marko
Illustrated by Michael Hackett

Publishing House
St. Louis

Copyright © 1979 by Concordia Publishing House
3558 South Jefferson Avenue, St. Louis, MO 63118

Printed in the United States of America

Library of Congress Cataloging in Publication Data

Marko, Katherine.
    God, when will I ever belong?

    SUMMARY: After a sequence of foster homes in which she was unhappy, 12-year-old Jeanie finds herself in a new one she dislikes for the same reasons.
    [1. Foster home care—Fiction.   2. Christian life—Fiction.
3. Adoption—Fiction]   I. Title.
PZ7.M3397Go   [Fic]   79-12244
ISBN 0-570-03624-0

To the memory of my parents,
Charles and Ellen McGlade

Chapter I

The June afternoon was hot, and Jeanie Hobbs was seething mad. It was time to use her old trick again. She'd made up her mind; she wasn't going to go on living with the Taylor family any longer.

They were all alike. All foster parents wanted foster kids for was to help with their work and be the means of collecting a check from the state.

Well, the Taylors weren't going to collect any more through her. They and their prissy daughter, Sue! Sue was always so prim and proper with her dark-brown hair combed just right and her neat clothes. They were both 12, but alongside Sue Jeanie felt big and clumsy with mouse-colored hair that was stiff and hard to manage.

The Taylors, Jeanie felt, were no better than the Bartleys who had three bratty boys or the Strunks with their twin babies. "They were always pushing more and more work on me," she grumbled.

Besides that the Taylors' house was a mile out of town. They had a garden, a corn patch, and chickens. There was more work to do here than at the other places.

"Just like now," she muttered. Here she was cleaning out a rotten, smelly hen house. She threw the shovel down with a thud. Wiping the perspiration from her face, she scratched her neck where the tiny chicken lice were bothering her. Then she tugged her rumpled blouse and red shorts loose from her clammy skin.

"Nuts! To the devil with this!" she said, and immediately clamped her mouth shut. She knew she shouldn't talk like that. But more and more lately she felt as though she had to say such things or she would explode. Then she stepped through the door.

"Are you finished, Jeanie?"

In her frustration she had not heard Mrs. Taylor come up to the hen house. She wondered if Mrs. Taylor heard what she said and was just ignoring it.

"No, and I'm not going to finish it," she snapped. "Let Sue do the rest of it."

"You know Sue has an allergy. She can't be near feathers."

Sure, Jeanie knew. She had heard about it often enough since she came to live here. But that didn't make it any easier to shovel out the chicken droppings and spray the hen house.

"We all have to do our share," Mrs. Taylor went on. "Sue was helping me in the garden." She didn't talk crossly. But her calm tone irritated Jeanie anyhow. "Here, let me finish it. You look awfully warm. Get yourself a glass of lemonade." Even her kindness rankled Jeanie.

As Mrs. Taylor reached out for the latch, she added, "We can't very well let this go over until tomorrow. Tomorrow's Sunday." She said that as though she thought Jeanie might have forgotten.

Now is the time, Jeanie thought, now. "I'm not going to church tomorrow," she announced bluntly.

"You aren't?" Mrs. Taylor stopped with the door half open. "Why not?"

Jeanie knew Mrs. Taylor was surprised, because they had all gone to church together since she lived there.

"Well . . . ," Jeanie hesitated. Now is the time, she told herself again, go on. Then lifting her chin, she plunged in. "Because I don't believe in God anyhow."

"Now, now," Mrs. Taylor began softly.

Why doesn't she get angry, Jeanie wondered. At the Home, where she was taken when she was only two, they aways warned, "Behave yourself. You are being placed with a good Christian family."

If that was so, why wasn't Mrs. Taylor angry when someone talked like that about God? She certainly wasn't like Mrs. Bartley. Mrs. Bartley was dumbstruck at first; then she blew up.

"How dare you talk like that! You get down on your knees and ask God's forgiveness."

Jeanie refused and Wham! Mrs. Bartley called the caseworker.

The same thing happened at the Strunks' place. Mrs. Strunk tried to cover all four of the twins' ears at one time. "Don't you dare talk like that in front of the children!"

So why did Mrs. Taylor act differently? Maybe she wants me to like living here, Jeanie thought. Well, she wasn't going to stay for good with anyone but her own real parents.

"You shouldn't talk like that," Mrs. Taylor began again.

Jeanie couldn't look at her. "Well, I don't believe in Him. I hate God." She ended with a shriek and ran off down through the fields to the creek.

Snatching off her sandals, she sat on the bank and dragged her feet from side to side through the cool, clear water. Well, she had done it. It had always worked before. Not only with the Bartleys and the Strunks, but with a couple of other foster families. They had all called the caseworker and she was returned to the Home in Emmetsville.

Lying on the creek bank she thought of Mr. and Mrs. Taylor at church tomorrow. Maybe folks would ask where *she* was. Maybe they would think the Taylors hadn't treated her right, and they would be embarrassed. Well, who cared? They weren't her parents. She wouldn't mind doing all kinds of work for her own parents. They would love her. So, let the Taylors be embarrassed and call the caseworker. That was why she had pulled her old trick.

But all she really wanted was to feel like she really belonged. You only belong to your real folks, Jeanie stubbornly argued with herself. And she wasn't going to be satisfied with foster parents, no matter who they were.

Finally she started back to the house.

"Where have you been?" Mrs. Taylor asked. "It's suppertime. Here, set the table." She handed Jeanie some cups and saucers.

"Where's Sue?" Jeanie asked, feeling put upon. Did the work just have to wait until she herself came back to do it?

"She's lying down," Mrs. Taylor answered. "The heat got to her."

"Good excuse," Jeanie muttered.

"Don't be fresh. Sue almost fainted."

O Lord, Jeanie thought. With summer just begun, I suppose I'll be stuck with all the work if Sue has to stop on

account of the heat.

She set the table in silence. The supper looked good, and there was plenty of it: steaming ears of corn, mashed potatoes, fried chicken, tossed salad, and stewed fruit for dessert. But her appetite was less than keen this evening.

Sue, still looking a little pale, came downstairs just as Mr. Taylor arrived home. He worked at Jake Jensen's hardware store in town. Beneath the nails of his broad fingers there were still traces of the oil and dust that coated the many tools. But a warm smile spread over his ruddy round face as he sat down at the table.

"Mmm-mm, that corn looks good," he said. "I guess it's time to set up the stand out front. See if we can sell some of it." He tucked his napkin into his collar and changed the subject. "How about you girls driving with Mom and me to the Dollar Mart after supper?"

The Dollar Mart was on the highway that ran into Emmetsville.

Sue lit up. "I'd like a new scarf."

"OK," Mr. Taylor said. "A nice bright blue one to match your eyes." He reached over and patter her shoulder. After a moment he turned to Jeanie. "Maybe you would like one too. You both can wear them to church tomorrow."

Jeanie was thinking: He didn't pat my shoulder. He just offered to get me a scarf to be polite. Then she said bluntly, "I'm not going to church."

Mr. Taylor looked surprised. "You're not? Why?"

"Because I don't believe in God anymore."

Beneath his furrowing brow Mr. Taylor's deep-brown eyes widened. "That's no way to talk, Jeanie."

Mrs. Taylor and Sue stopped eating and looked at each other.

"Well, I don't," Jeanie blurted. "I hate God."

She wasn't prepared for Mr. Taylor's calm response, "Why?"

"Because—because I asked Him so often to help me find my real parents and . . ." Her voice trailed off. She felt her bottom lip tremble, and she shut her eyes to hold back the tears. I won't cry! I can't cry! she told herself over and over. After a moment she jerked her head up and said as sarcastically as she could, "God's too important to worry about a kid like me."

No one answered. The Taylors sat eating their dinner mechanically. They seemed stunned, lost in their own thoughts. I know what they're thinking, Jeanie thought. Good. It's working. If I've got them pegged, I'll be gone by the end of next week.

After she'd helped with the dishes, Jeanie went up to her room and fell across the bed. It was a nice room, nicer than the room she'd shared with four other girls at the Home. Flouncy yellow curtains hung at the windows, which overlooked open fields. Her bed was at the wall opposite the window, and it had a matching yellow bedspread. Jeanie had loved the room on first sight and had wondered how Mrs. Taylor had known that yellow was her favorite color. Just chance, she'd told herself. Surely the Taylors hadn't decorated that room in yellow just for her? It was a room every girl dreamed of having back at the Home, but it could trap you into thinking that you really belonged.

"But I don't belong," Jeanie cried to herself. Oh, it was all very nice, but she wasn't about to be fooled by any of it. The Taylors were like all the rest.

She walked over to her dresser. On her first evening there, Sue had showed her the pressed rose petals in the drawers. Jeanie loved the fragrance and often lifted her clothes out just to smell the petals. She would miss those roses, now that she was going back to the Home.

"What's going to happen to me?" she asked her reflection in the mirror. "When will I ever belong?"

A tap sounded on her door. It was Sue. "Jeanie, we're getting ready to leave. Don't you want to come with us?"

Yes, yes, I'd love to go, but instead she remained silent.

"Jeanie?" Sue called.

Still Jeanie wouldn't answer.

"I guess she's asleep, Mom."

"All right," Mrs. Taylor answered. "Don't disturb her then."

Jeanie stood quietly by the window watching as the Taylors' old Ford rumbled out of the driveway, past the pink rambler that climbed the trellis at the front gate. That was the color of the scarf she would have picked if she had gone to the Dollar Mart.

Maybe I should have gone with them. . . . Oh well, it's too late now. Too late for anything.

Chapter II

Jeanie wondered how she would face the Taylors. What would she say to them? If they yelled or scolded, she could handle that by just getting angry herself. She had been rude before, and stubborn about chores. Like the time she did the dishes but wouldn't put them away. Or when she ironed her own blouses but wouldn't hang them up, and other things. Maybe she should just stay up here in her room. Then she heard footsteps and a tap on her door.

"Jeanie?" It was Sue. "Are you awake yet?"

Before thinking twice, she answered, "Yes. Come on in."

Sue snapped on the wall switch and stood just inside the door. The bright light blinded Jeanie for a moment, and she put up her hand to shield her eyes.

When she didn't say anything, Sue asked, "How do you like it?" She gestured to the blue scarf tied neatly around her neck.

"It's pretty," Jeanie answered, hoping her eyes weren't telltale red from crying. She was angry with herself now for not going along. She had spent a miserable time alone.

But Sue was smiling. From behind her back she produced another scarf. "This is the color you wanted, isn't it?"

It was a soft pink, just like the rambler. Sue remembered. Quickly Jeanie wiped that thought out of her mind. No one was going to make her go soft.

"Yes, that's right," she answered evenly.

Then getting up off the bed she took the scarf from Sue. Tying it around her neck, she looked in the mirror. It was pretty.

Sue went towards her. "It looks nice on you."

Before Jeanie turned from the mirror, though, she caught Sue's face reflected there. Sue looked uncertain about something. As Jeanie watched her, Sue started for the door, stopped, and glanced back.

"You didn't mean what you said, did you?" She hesitated. "You know, about hating God?"

Anger swept through Jeanie. So that was it. They were just trying to get to her. She pulled off the scarf and threw it on the bed. "I don't want it," she snapped.

Sue looked at it and backed to the door. "I'm sorry," she said softly and went out.

Jeanie was immediately sorry herself. Why did she always act like that—bad-tempered and quick with her mouth? Once Mrs. Selby at the Home told her she should try to cultivate the habit of saying "I'm sorry" and "Thank you." She had a terrible time saying either one.

Maybe Sue had only wanted to be nice. Maybe she wasn't trying to get around her at all. Well, she *could* go downstairs and say "I'm sorry" to Sue and "Thank you" to Mr. Taylor. But they might think they were winning her over, and she wasn't going to let them think that.

She paced across the room and then back—back and forth like the old rooster as he ran along the fence every time he saw her coming with the chicken feed. She switched off the light and looked out at the fireflies blinking over the darkened fields. It was too early to go to bed. Besides, she would like to watch television for a while. Well, apologizing to Sue *was* a good excuse to go downstairs. She'd go bananas if she stayed in her room much longer.

Picking up the scarf, she tied it around her neck again. The stairway led into the living room. Sue and her parents, seated there, must have heard her before they saw her because they turned and smiled as she approached them. But before any of them could say anything, Jeanie went towards Sue.

"I'm sorry I acted so rotten," she said, and meant it. Mrs. Selby would have been proud of her. Then quickly she turned to Mr. and Mrs. Taylor. "Thank you for the scarf."

"Oh, you're welcome," Mr. Taylor said. "It looks nice on you."

Mrs. Taylor pulled a chair forward. "Yes, it does. Now come and watch this program with us."

Well, that was done easily enough, Jeanie thought, not nearly as difficult as she had expected. They all seemed pleased with her behavior. Maybe they thought she was softening up. But she wasn't. She might have to show them later that her intention of getting away was just as strong as ever. But she might as well enjoy the rest of the evening. She had enough clashes for one day.

The week went by slowly. True to his statement, Mr. Taylor set up the stand out front to sell sweet corn. Jeanie said she would paint the sign for it. She liked to paint. So she covered the whole sign with white and then lettered it: "Fresh corn—75¢ a dozen."

When the canvas canopy was adjusted over the stand, she and Sue carried out the ears of corn and stacked them neatly.

After lunch Mrs. Taylor set a little box of change beside the corn and said, "Now you girls can sit here in the shade and take care of the customers."

"Do you think there'll be any?" Jeanie asked.

"Oh yes," Mrs. Taylor answered, turning back to the house. "Today's Friday. Weekends are pretty good for sales."

Jeanie looked down the road which curved around their corn patch and ran west. The afternoon was quiet and drowsy, with the locusts making their sawing sound in the weeds along the road.

After a while a car stopped. Jeanie jumped to her feet.

"May I have the first customer?" she asked.

Sue nodded. "Sure. I'll take the second and you take the third and so on."

A woman leaned from the car window. "One dozen, please."

Jeanie bagged 12 ears, took the customer's dollar and gave her 25 cents change. When the customer left, Jeanie laughed happily. "That was fun." She liked being a saleslady.

They sold four dozen that day and five on Saturday. Jeanie enjoyed the whole thing.

Then came Saturday evening, and her spirits dashed to earth again. Would there be a hassel about church tomorrow? she wondered.

But Mrs. Taylor only asked her about it casually and added, "A person always feels better about problems after going to church."

"No," Jeanie answered. "I still hate God." She made her

voice glib, as though the whole thing were unimportant. But deep inside of her she felt that what she said was true. Why should she love Somebody who wouldn't even help her? If God could do everything, why was He so stubborn about helping her to find her real parents?

Mr. Taylor didn't make any comment. Neither did Sue. But Jeanie caught the knowing look that passed between them. She ignored it.

Then Mr. Taylor dismissed the subject by saying, "We better get going if we want to shop at the Dollar Mart."

This time Jeanie went with them. She liked roaming along the counters, smelling the colognes, looking inside the books, popping a wide-brimmed hat on her head and laughing at her reflection in the mirror. But she stood silently by as Sue selected a tortoise barrette and handed it to her father.

Mr. Taylor smiled and patted Sue's shoulder as usual. Jeanie winced at the affectionate touch. But she told herself that if her own father were there he would do the same thing for her.

Then Mr. Taylor turned to her. "Wouldn't you like one too?"

"Maybe," she half-yielded. Why not? she thought. She would only be spiting herself if she refused. Then she picked up a pink plastic one studded with tiny white daisies. "This is pretty."

Mr. Taylor put the barrettes in the shopping cart along with the material and thread Mrs. Taylor wanted and other things like trash bags, paper towels, and shampoo.

Mr. Taylor usually brought the grocery order home on Monday evening after shopping on the way from work. But with all the shopping, on Tuesday Mrs. Taylor discovered she had no bacon or flour. "I don't know how I forgot to put them on the list for Mr. Taylor yesterday," she said and asked Jeanie to walk down to the general store to the south of them.

"That's a good mile, and it's hot," Jeanie protested.

"I know," Mrs. Taylor said, "but I really need both things or I wouldn't ask you to go."

Jeanie remained stubborn. "Why doesn't Sue go?"

"You know the heat gets to her."

"OK, OK, I'll go. I'm too thick-skinned for the heat to soak through me, I know."

"Now, Jeanie, don't talk like that."

But Jeanie had snatched the change purse and note and was stomping off down the path. All the way to the store and back she fumed inwardly. "Always the same—do this, do that, whatever the kids in the families are too good to do," she muttered.

When she returned, she slapped the items and change down on the kitchen table and then stalked out to the front porch. Flopping down on a chair, she wiped the perspiration from her face and neck.

Sue came out a few moments later with a can of soda pop for her. "Here, this will make you feel better."

"Nothing will make me feel better."

"I'm sorry," Sue began, "I would have gone if . . ."

"If there wasn't a foster kid around," Jeanie finished.

Sue bristled. "I wasn't going to say that at all."

"But you meant it."

Sue stamped her foot. "I did not."

"That's what you say."

Sue's face was growing red. "Oh, why don't you go back to that Home and leave us alone? You only make my mother all upset with your—your . . ." Sue sputtered to a stop.

Jeanie had a fiendish thought—good, Sue's fighting back. I'm not the only one with a hot temper. Now I won't have to feel guilty.

Just then Mrs. Taylor came through the doorway. "Sue, Jeanie, stop this quarreling at once." She looked disturbed.

"She started it," Jeanie said.

"I did not," Sue defended herself, but she was near tears. Jeanie could see the shiny look in her eyes. And she began to feel guilty after all. Phooey! If there was anything she hated it was feeling guilty. She thumped down the porch steps, ready to yell out a bad word, but she bit it back in time. She couldn't go around using such language. What if she had a habit like that when she found her parents?

Instead she yelled back, "I'm going to sit at the stand."

Then she heard Mrs. Taylor tell Sue, "I told you to be patient with her. Believe me, Sue, I know her problem."

Phooey! Jeanie thought again, how could she know? But she did wonder at the patience Mrs. Taylor showed her. What was behind it anyhow?

Then Sue answered, "Yes, but does she know mine?"

What was Sue's problem? The heat getting to her? Big

deal! The heat bothered lots of people. Oh, the heck with everything.

She plunked herself down on the lawn chair. It would look dumb, she knew, sitting at an empty stand. But she didn't care. She had to think.

Chapter III

Jeanie sat sulking at the empty corn stand for about five minutes. Then she picked up a twig and, bending over, scratched her name in the dirt at her feet. She put her name in everything she owned, too—her books (she only had three), her coat, her handbag, even her little yellow change purse.

She was just straightening up when she heard Mrs. Taylor speak to Sue on the porch. But she couldn't distinguish the words. Finally Mrs. Taylor came down the porch steps and called to her.

"Jeanie, come here. I must talk to you."

Jeanie didn't move. "I don't want to."

Mrs. Taylor raised her voice. "I don't care what you want. Come to the porch this instant."

That was the first time Jeanie ever heard Mrs. Taylor speak in an angry tone. She must really be sore. Slowly Jeanie rose from the chair and started forward. Dragging each step, she went up the walk.

When she reached the porch, Mrs. Taylor told Sue, "Go inside."

Sue protested.

Mrs. Taylor raised her voice again. "I said go inside, Sue."

Jeanie slouched over to the chair where she had been sitting earlier and sank down into it.

Mrs. Taylor looked long at her. "All right, I've tried to be fair, but I've reached the end of my patience. What is it you want?"

Jeanie didn't answer.

Twisting her hands, Mrs. Taylor walked to the end of the porch. "I know some foster homes aren't the best . . ." Oh, Jeanie knew that very well. One boy was brought back to the Home because his foster parents left him alone without food. Mrs. Taylor was saying, "but we—Mr. Taylor and I—always thought we could be good to anyone who stayed with us." She turned and looked searchingly again at Jeanie. "Aren't we as good as the other foster parents who took care of you?"

Still Jeanie didn't answer.

"I know you had trouble at some of the other places where you stayed," Mrs. Taylor went on.

Oh, she had to bring that up, Jeanie thought, and was about to tell her that was none of her business.

But Mrs. Taylor continued, "We thought things would work out differently for us, but I guess I was wrong."

Jeanie still remained silent.

Now Mrs. Taylor pressed her. "Did you like any of the others better than us?"

Jeanie fidgeted uneasily. "I didn't like any of them."

"Well," Mrs. Taylor said, "I thought that you'd like us after a while if we treated you well. But I—I guess I failed you somehow or other."

"You said that—I didn't."

Mrs. Taylor seemed to ignore the jibe. "Do you really want to leave and go back to the Home?"

Jeanie hunched around in her chair so that Mrs. Taylor couldn't see her face. "Yes. Yes, that's what I want." She was feeling mixed up again, so she made her voice as surly as she could.

"Oh, Jeanie," Mrs. Taylor said. She sounded defeated. "All right then, I'll call Mrs. Keyes at the Home tomorrow and speak to her." She went inside.

Jeanie just sat there. She didn't know whether she felt good or bad about it. Then she started thinking about the Home. What would the little freckled-faced girl named Molly be doing now? Molly always wished someone would adopt her. And how about Paul Krampf, who looked like a horse when he laughed?

She got up and wandered down through the fields to the creek. Lying on its bank, she remembered the last time she lay there—the day she told Mrs. Taylor she hated God. She jumped to her feet and started back to the house. She had enough on her mind. She didn't want to start feeling guilty about God.

No one said anything further about the quarrel, and Jeanie didn't apologize to Sue this time. Sue was just as much to blame as she, she felt, so let Sue be sorry. Mrs. Taylor acted as though nothing happened, but she looked a little sad.

Finally, when they were doing the supper dishes, Sue said, "I'm sorry we quarreled. I don't feel good about it at all."

"I'm sorry too," Jeanie said without looking at Sue. But she felt better almost immediately.

Just then Mr. Taylor went through the kitchen. He stopped at the door. "Why don't you girls go out and pick some corn for the stand tomorrow. It'll be cooler now than tomorrow morning."

"OK, Dad," Sue answered. "How about it, Jeanie?"

"Sure." It would be a way of spending part of the evening, Jeanie thought. She was getting fidgety. She wondered what she would be doing if she were with her own parents. Maybe she'd even have brothers and sisters. Maybe they would play some games or sing around a piano. She missed the piano at the Home. Sometimes she wished the Taylors had one. But there was no sense wishing that now. She'd be leaving soon.

"Come on," Sue broke in on her thoughts and was handing her a basket.

As they went through the door, Jeanie caught the scent of the rambler. "Mmmm, those roses smell pretty."

The evening was nice, but the space between the rows of corn was still steamy from the heat of the day. A robin chirruped on its way to its nest, and a bat swooped low. Sue shrieked and Jeanie ducked. Then they both laughed. The quarrel seemed forgotten.

Just as they had filled their baskets, a train whistle sounded across the valley. Jeanie stopped, set down her basket, and covered her ears.

Sue looked at her in surprise. "Why're you going that?"

"Because I don't want to hear the train whistle."

"Oh, I do. I love to hear them. They always make me think of faraway places."

"That's why," Jeanie said. The train whistle sounded again. She clapped her hands harder over her ears, and her words sounded as though she were talking into a barrel. "I don't want to think of faraway places. I'll never be going to any of them." Only more foster homes, she thought, one after the other. Always sharing someone else's family, never her own.

She envied the dreamy look in Sue's eyes. But the next instant a shadow wiped it away and Sue was saying, "But I'm always afraid that someday when I'm not home anymore I'll be terribly homesick every time I hear a train whistle."

Jeanie could understand that, but she herself wouldn't have to worry about it. "Well, I'm not home. I can't ever be homesick for what I never had."

There was a moment of awkward silence. Then Sue timidly put her hand on Jeanie's arm. "You could be home here. You could belong to our family."

Jeanie shook off Sue's hand and looked away. "Yeah, I know, but I'd still be sharing someone else's home." Her thoughts turned sour again.

Sue turned silently and started out of the corn patch. For a moment Jeanie listened to the sounds on the evening air. The train was gone. A plane zoomed overhead, but its swoosh couldn't stir up dreams as a train whistle could. She picked up her basket and followed Sue.

When she caught up, Sue said, "Jeanie? Now don't get mad."

"At what?"

"At what I'm going to say."

"OK, I won't get mad."

"Well, your parents gave you away," Sue ventured. "What if you found out they didn't want you?"

Jeanie could feel the heat crawling up her neck. But she had promised not to be mad. "They gave me away because at that time they couldn't take care of me." Most of the kids in Harvey Home were there because their parents were dead or so poor they couldn't keep them. And that's why she was there. She would never let herself think that her parents didn't want her. "I'm big enough now to take care of myself," she added. "I know they would want me now."

Sue nodded and smiled. "They would."

Jeanie hoped she was right.

Chapter IV

Wednesday dawned hot and humid. But chores had to be done regardless. Jeanie fed the chickens and gathered the eggs. She made her bed and straightened her room. She also usually shared the chores of dusting and dishes with Sue, but today Mrs. Taylor told Sue to do those tasks alone.

"And you, Jeanie, you can weed the beets and carrots in the garden. They're getting a nice start, and I don't want them choked by weeds and grass springing up between them."

Jeanie was about to complain, "Sure, Sue can stay in out of the sun," but she held her tongue. She wasn't going to be here much longer anyhow.

At least Mrs. Taylor always did the laundry herself. Jeanie hated slopping around in water. From the garden she watched until Mrs. Taylor had hung up the last sheet and pillow case. Then she got up from her knees in the garden. She gave the plot of vegetables a careless glance. It was good enough. She rubbed her hands down her jeans and strolled back to the house. Mrs. Taylor, looking weary, was about to sit in the canvas chair near the back door. Jeanie sank down on the steps.

"Sue," Mrs. Taylor called, "bring out that pitcher of orange drink in the refrigerator." Then she said to Jeanie, "We'll take it easy until lunchtime."

As she poured them each a drink, the clinking of the ice cubes sounded so cool. A big elm tree shaded the area, but the air hung heavy and not a leaf moved.

Sue, holding her glass carefully, lowered herself slowly to the grass beside her mother's chair. "I hate this weather," she said.

Mrs. Taylor reached over and patted Sue's shoulder. "Well, rest yourself now, dear."

Again Jeanie envied the affection given to Sue. "Why doesn't anyone ever pat my shoulder?" she asked bluntly. "Am I poison or something?"

"Now, Jeanie," Mrs. Taylor said, "you musn't feel that way."

"Well, I must be—like a snake or—or a vulture."

"Jeanie," Mrs. Taylor began again.

Then Sue leaned forward. "Maybe it's because you always seem so angry. No one ever gets that near—to you." Her voice dropped off to a hesitant low tone.

"I am not always angry," Jeanie flared.

"I didn't *say* you were."

"But you meant it."

Mrs. Taylor put up her hands. "Girls, girls, don't start again."

"Oh, she just wants to fight," Sue said, getting to her feet.

"I do not."

"Yes you do, and you *are* always angry, so there."

Mrs. Taylor rose and put her hands firmly on Sue's arms, steering her away. "It's too hot to argue, and I just can't stand your quarreling."

But Sue's face was flushed now and her shoulders were rigid. She walked over to Jeanie and glared down at her. "All you do is pity yourself. All you think of is your real parents. No one else is as good as they are. How do you know they're any good at all?"

"Don't you talk about my mother and father!"

Mrs. Taylor stood between them. "Jeanie's right, Sue. You have no right to say anything about anyone's parents."

For a moment Sue's breath came short. Then her eyes lost their flash and her shoulders slumped. Again she was meek little Sue. "But, Mother, she doesn't think you and Dad are as good as they are. Why doesn't she, just once, see that others are kind . . ."

Jeanie didn't want to hear any more. Sue's words were hard to swallow. "Shut up—just shut up," she shouted and gulped down her drink.

Then pushing herself to her feet she strode across the yard. "I'll go stack the corn in the stand," she called over her shoulder. Let them think she didn't care. But she did wish this quarrel hadn't happened. That morning she had thought she could almost be a model foster child for her time remaining here. But now it had all gone up in smoke. She wished she could leave right now.

Well, even though she hadn't planned the quarrels, she didn't have to worry about getting away from the Taylors now. She was sure of that. When Mrs. Taylor called her for lunch she went in immediately. No sense in causing any more hard feelings. But the afternoon dragged endlessly. Only two customers stopped by.

Sue sat at the stand with her but kept her nose in a book. Jeanie wished she would talk, but she guessed Sue felt they'd only argue again. Maybe they would. She couldn't help being jealous of someone with a family. So everyone thought she was just ill-tempered and hard to manage.

The afternoon was almost spent when Sue at last turned to her and said, "I'm sorry I spoke about your parents. I love my mother and father and I know you love yours even though you don't know them. I'd feel awful if I couldn't find my parents, so I know how you feel."

Jeanie shook her head slowly. "No, you don't." Then she added softly, "You never could." She gulped hard. It was so awful to have that lump in your throat that you can't swallow down. And her eyes stung. Holding them real wide open would help. Because she wasn't going to cry, no matter what.

She wondered what they would all think if they knew she had cried that evening when she didn't go to the Dollar Mart with them.

"Well," Sue said, "I just wanted to apologize for what I said."

Then she returned to her book and went back into her silence.

Jeanie had given up on any more customers coming when a truck stopped.

"Is this the Taylor house?" the driver called to them.

Sue jumped up. "Yes, it is."

"Well, I've got a package here for a Miss Susan Taylor."

"Oh," Sue squealed delightedly, "that's me."

"OK, you can sign for it."

Jeanie glanced at the package. It was quite a large box, all secured with brown paper tape.

"I better carry it up to the house for you," the driver told them. "It's pretty heavy."

Sue almost danced beside him. But Jeanie didn't move. Sue looked over her shoulder and then ran back to her. "Come on, Jeanie," she invited, "let's see what it is." Again their quarrel seemed forgotten.

The truck driver set the box on the porch and left.

"Mother, Mother," Sue called, "come look what I got."

"I'll help you carry it inside," Jeanie offered. She tilted it slightly so that she could tuck her fingers under the edge. Sue caught the other side. Just as they were trying to turn the knob, Mrs. Taylor opened the door. Then as they set the box on the coffee table, she read the return address.

"Why, it's from your Uncle Edward," she said. Her eyes looked happy. Edward was her brother. Pulling the box flaps up, Sue looked in and then put her hands up to her cheeks. "It's a record player." She grabbed out the little card and read it out loud. "Happy Belated Birthday. Sorry I wasn't on time."

Sue put the card on the table. "Gosh, my birthday was in April. I forgot all about it."

Wow! What a present, Jeanie was thinking. No one could tell her that relatives made no difference. How about two weeks ago when Sue's grandparents and an uncle and aunt and three older cousins came to visit? They all had supper out under the big elm tree. A long table was laden with the dishes and casseroles the relatives had brought plus all the things Mrs. Taylor had cooked and baked. Long after they had eaten, everyone sat at the table talking about funny things that happened in the past. They all had such a good time.

How could she ever look forward to something like that when she didn't even know whom she belonged to?

Sue was opening another flat cardboard container. Inside was a record with a label reading, "Happy Birthday."

They were playing it for the tenth time when Mr. Taylor arrived home from work. "Better close the stand if you're through for the day," he said, but he was as excited as they were about the gift.

Jeanie ran out to the stand, took the change box, and let the canvas curtain roll down over the front from the canopy.

Just as she went back into the house, she heard Mr. Taylor

saying, "We must get some records for it on Saturday evening." Jeanie knew he meant when they went to the Dollar Mart. She wondered if she would be going with them.

But at suppertime Mrs. Taylor announced, "I called the Harvey Home today. Mrs. Keyes said if I wanted you taken back it's all right with her."

Mr. Taylor put down his fork and looked thoughtful. After a long moment he exhaled, puffing out his ruddy cheeks, and said, "Why couldn't you be happy with us, Jeanie?"

Jeanie shrugged. "You're not my parents; that's all I know." She made her face a mask so they couldn't tell what she was thinking. Then she pushed her plate away. She didn't feel like eating anymore. No one was going to understand how she felt anyway. Mr. Taylor wagged his head and picked up his fork again. There, he was going to enjoy his supper without bothering about her anymore. That made her feel worse.

"Mrs. Keyes said you should finish out the week here," Mrs. Taylor told her. "On Monday afternoon she'll send the caseworker with the papers for me to sign. You can go back with her." She looked sad as she finished.

Jeanie found herself wishing that Mrs. Taylor would be relieved and happy instead, just as Mrs. Stark and Mrs. Bartley were when she left them.

Well, another four days and she'd be back at the Home, and then what? She never felt mixed up like this when she left the other foster homes.

Chapter V

The next morning, after they had breakfast and Mr. Taylor had left for work, Sue handed the newspaper to Jeanie. "Look, it says that there is an agency or something—that finds adopted children's real parents for them."

Jeanie snatched the paper and read swiftly. ". . . Mrs. Jackson, head of the agency, herself adopted when she was two years old, feels that everyone has a right to know his or her biological parents. . . ."

Jeanie stumbled over the word biological—she guessed it meant your real parents—and then skimmed on, reading as fast as she could.

Sue was saying, "Maybe you could write to that lady and she would help you."

Jeanie reached the end of the write-up. ". . . a person has to be 18 years of age before such action could be taken."

Eighteen!

"But I'm only 12," she exploded. Crumpling the page into a ball, she threw it to the floor.

Sue's mouth fell open, and then she reached down and picked up the paper. Spreading it out timidly, she read the whole write-up. "I'm sorry, Jeanie; I didn't read it all before."

Jeanie didn't look at her. "Oh, that's all right." But she felt as though someone had smiled at her and then slapped her hard across the face.

She and Sue did their chores, and the first chance they got to play the record player, they started it up. Mrs. Taylor laughed.

"We surely do have to get some records or you'll wear the grooves right off that one," she said. She always seemed happy when she saw them doing something together.

Jeanie wondered if Mrs. Taylor still hoped she would stay.

"You'll come with us to pick out some new records, won't you," Sue asked her, "on Saturday evening?"

"Maybe," was all she felt like saying.

The afternoon was another scorcher. A few bees buzzed in the flowers along the walk, and someone's hunting hound bayed mournfully several times. Sitting at the stand, Jeanie watched the tree branches, hoping they would move just a little to prove there was some air stirring. But the sultry day dragged on.

They had several customers and there were only two dozen ears left when an old car stopped. Two thin women got out. They wore flowered cotton dresses made in the same style, but one was tall and pinch-faced, the other, short with round, full cheeks.

"Mmmm—how is your corn, young ladies?" the tall one asked in a crisp manner.

How were they going to answer that dumb question, Jeanie was thinking, when Sue spoke up a little hesitantly.

"It's—it's fine."

"Well, we'll see for ourselves, if you don't mind." And the woman's long skinny fingers ripped the husks halfway down three of the ears. "Mmm—seems all right. Don't you think so, Clara?"

"Oh yes, much better than some we bought last week."

"*That*," the taller woman said, "was out-and-out cheating. Scarcely a decent kernel on any of the cobs. Well, we'll take a half-dozen ears."

"A half-dozen!" Jeanie said. *Good gosh! Only six ears after all that fuss.*

"Yes, one half-dozen, I said. Is there anything wrong with that?"

"Oh no," Sue put in quickly, "nothing's wrong." She was reaching for three more ears. She was about to pick up the half-stripped ears, but must have thought better of it. Instead she took three fresh ones and put them into the bag.

The woman paid with a quarter, a dime, and three pennies. Sue looked at the coins and began to count them.

"That's 38 cents, half of 75," the tall woman said tartly, but she was looking searchingly at Jeanie.

Jeanie didn't like her from the start, but she told Sue, "That's right." Why was the woman looking at her like that?

Then point-blank the woman asked her, "What is your name?"

"Jeanie." And that was all she was going to tell the nosy old thing.

The one called Clara took the bag and turned back to the car.

"Wait a minute," the tall one said. "This young lady reminds me of someone. She blinked her steely, close-set eyes as though trying to remember. Then she said, "Oh yes, a fellow Arthur once knew. Arthur's our brother," she explained shortly, "and he used to bring this—this fellow home for supper sometimes. Can't say I was overjoyed at the idea. His name was Melvin something or other. I can't remember rightly. He ran off with a girl who was new around here."

Jeanie leaned forward. If she looked like this fellow, she might be related to him. Maybe the girl he ran off with was her mother. But the woman spoke so disagreeably about them, Jeanie was afraid to ask anything further. The woman might give her some awful news, like the man was in jail or something.

The woman was still staring at her. She could bore a hole through you with that look, Jeanie was thinking. Then the woman went on, "You resemble him a great deal—the same yellowish eyes."

"Oh, that was 12 or 13 years ago," Clara said. "We've never seen him since."

"No, Arthur said they moved to Regents Hill."

Jeanie took a chance and asked, "Where are they now?"

"I don't know and I don't care," the woman said with a sniff. "Probably still in Regents Hill. Come, Clara."

They minced their way back to the car. Sue and Jeanie watched them out of sight. Then Sue said, "Such old gossips. You'd think no one ever saw yellow eyes before."

"They're tawny," Jeanie said, but she didn't care much about her eyes just then. If what the gossipy woman said was true, the man named Melvin could be her father. If she went to Regents Hill, she might find him, and if she found him, and he was her father, she most likely would find her mother there too. She must go to Regents Hill, but how? It was between 15 and 20 miles to the west.

The afternoon was almost spent. "Let's close up," Sue said. "It's getting late."

When they told Mrs. Taylor about the two women, she seemed troubled by the news. "They must be the Jody sisters. I think it's dreadful for women that age to go around stirring up hopes in anyone. Just put it out of your head, Jeanie. I wouldn't want to see you hurt."

That sounded strange. How could she be hurt if it were only gossip? And if it were true and she found her parents, that would be wonderful. It was silly for Mrs. Taylor to worry.

But Jeanie was getting all keyed up, and by the time Mr. Taylor came home from work, she blurted out the incident to him and asked, "Do you think maybe the man named Melvin could be my father?"

"Oh, that's foolish," he said with a short laugh. "Why can't you settle down and be content with . . ."

"Because I want to find my parents." He should know that by now, she thought.

"That's a lot of stupid nonsense. You'll never find them."

She was hurt by his tone. He had never spoken to her like that before. "You're wrong. I will find them."

"Don't tell me I'm wrong," he scolded. "Do you want your life to add up to a lot of wild goose chases?"

She looked at Sue, who only that morning gave her the newspaper write-up about finding one's parents. But now Sue just looked down at her hands. Mrs. Taylor was silent too.

"Just put finding this man out of your head," Mr. Taylor finished.

Jeanie said nothing further. There'd be no use wishing Mr. Taylor would offer to drive her to Regents Hill or to ask him to. She'd have to go by bus, and she would have to go the very next day. She'd only be here until Monday. She couldn't waste any time, but she had no bus fare. The only place she knew of to get the cash was the little corn box in the cupboard. And that belonged to Mrs. Taylor.

Would she dare to take enough to get her to Regents Hill? She had never stolen anything in her life. But she wouldn't steal it; she would just borrow it.

Chapter VI

Jeanie knew it wasn't going to be easy to get away unnoticed. In the first place, there had to be a time when it would be safe to sneak the money out of the corn box. Then she would have to leave without arousing suspicion.

Early in the morning she'd run the chance of Mr. Taylor seeing her. He always got up early and made ready to go to work while Mrs. Taylor perked the coffee and fried his bacon and eggs. The girls rose a little later, but in time to eat with him.

Today, as usual, Jeanie hurried out to feed the chickens. They clucked busily as they ran helter-skelter pecking at the feed she tossed in front of them. Instead of spreading it around by throwing handfuls here and there, she emptied the pan in one wide swing to get it over with. Her nerves felt so tight they could screech. She hoped nobody would notice how tense and fidgety she was.

The other chores kept her close to Mrs. Taylor and Sue for most of the morning. But shortly after noon Mrs. Taylor said Sue was looking rather pale. "Maybe you better take a little rest." Then she told Jeanie to get a pan of apples from the cellar. "I want to make some apple sauce," she said as she settled down to peel them in the shade of the elm tree.

Jeanie went inside again. The house was quiet. Sue was upstairs taking a rest as her mother suggested. Always resting and taking vitamins, Jeanie thought. Sue should be as strong as an ox. Well, she couldn't dwell on Sue's health now.

She went to the cupboard and took down the corn box. There were several one-dollar bills and some coins in it. She took two of the bills and slipped them in the little yellow change purse in the pocket of her blue shorts. Then quickly she stole upstairs and got her old suede handbag with the fringe on it from her room. Into it she put the change purse, a fresh handkerchief, her comb, and a little mirror. She added a pencil and a piece of paper just in case someone gave her an address or a name or something she would want to copy down.

She wished she could put on her pink-striped, perma-press dress, her new scarf, and her white sandals. It would be nice, if she found her father, to be all dressed up for him. But Mrs. Taylor would surely want to know why she had changed. Both girls aways wore shorts or jeans around the house.

Downstairs again, she secreted the handbag under the newspaper lining of a basket. Then with the basket on her arm she went out.

"I guess I'll pick some corn for the stand," she told Mrs. Taylor.

"Oh, I thought most of the stalks were pretty well stripped."

"Maybe I'll find a few more ears," Jeanie said.

Mrs. Taylor dropped the last peeled apple into the bowl on her lap. "Well," she said, "it's quite warm in the sun. You should wait until evening."

"Oh, I don't mind the heat like Sue," Jeanie told her. "It doesn't bother me." That really was a fib. She didn't like the heat.

"You're lucky, Jeanie. Is Sue lying down?"

"Yes, she's resting," Jeanie answered, and quickly began to move away.

Once in the corn patch, she put down the basket. Grabbing up her handbag, she hurried southward through the rows to the road where it ran west towards Regents Hill.

It should be about 1:30 now, she guessed. And the bus was due at 1:45. There was no bus shelter on this stretch of road, and she wished there were a tree nearby to shade her from the heat of the sun.

Then a little yellow flash caught her eye, a butterfly. She liked butterflies, but she liked them flying the way God—she wasn't going to think about God—the way they were meant to be.

She remembered little freckle-faced Molly at the Home. Molly was always trying to catch butterflies on the lawn of the Home. One day, when Jeanie was watching her, she did catch one. She held it by the wings a moment, then let it flutter a little, and then caught it again. Its poor wings were smudged where Molly's sweaty little fingers had held them too tightly. Jeanie made her let it go. It could hardly fly.

"Look, you hurt its wings," she said severely to Molly. "How would you like someone to cut off your legs so you couldn't walk?"

Molly's big eyes welled up, and Jeanie was immediately sorry. She shouldn't have said it in that way. Molly didn't hurt the butterfly just to be mean. She really liked it. Jeanie pressed her close and gave her a tissue to dry her eyes.

After that Molly always hung around Jeanie. But she was awfully pesty when she got to wishing she could be adopted.

"Wouldn't you like to be adopted?" she'd ask Jeanie.

"No," Jeanie always answered. "I want my own parents, not somebody else's." Then she asked Molly, "Why do you want to be adopted?"

"Because then I'll have a family."

"Don't be so dumb. They'll be just like a foster family—it won't really be your own."

"I can make believe it is."

"Aw . . ." Jeanie didn't go any further. Why bother? Let the kid be happy, she thought.

She herself was going to solve her own problem this very day, if she could. She didn't have to wait long for the bus. She looked up the road to see it making the turn at the end of the corn patch. She waved both her arms to flag it down.

As she paid her fare, her hand trembled. Just looking at the money gave her an awful feeling. But she intended to pay it back. So she shoved the thought to the back of her mind. It would be fun to enjoy the ride, just looking out at the scenery flashing by. But the meeting with her father—she made believe it was really going to happen—well, that took some thought. She had to prepare in her mind what she would say.

Should she just go up to him and say, "Hello, Daddy. I'm Jeanie?" No, he'd just think she was crazy. Be a little shy and say, "I'm glad to meet you, Daddy. I'm hoping you'll like me?" No, that sounded more like Sue than it did like her. What then? She'd have to wait and see. But, all too soon, the bus was

pulling into town and stopping at the curb of a seedy, run-down street.

"Regents Hill," the bus driver called. He slid around in his seat to watch the passengers get off. A stout woman in a wrinkled green-print dress was first. She held the others up as she slowly planted her heavy feet both together on each step. Two men in overalls followed her. They all crossed in front of the bus and went down the other side of the street.

Jeanie got off last. A lonely feeling swept over her when the bus driver shut the door. The bus moved off, blowing the hot exhaust air across her legs.

She looked around. There was a close, hot-looking little restaurant next to a steamy-windowed laundromat. Then came a small appliance repair shop. In its window a toaster, an iron, and a waffle maker, all coated with dust, sat on a length of faded, fly-specked green paper. Then her glance reached a secondhand store with a collection of used and battered items piled any old way. One place was more dismal than the other.

She wished the bus had stopped in a better part of town. Maybe her father lived on a nicer street.

Then she caught sight of a barber pole. She had once heard that a barber knows almost everyone in town, or at least about them. The door stood open and she leaned forward to peek in. On a bench along one side sat two straggly looking boys. A third one was in the chair. He seemed to be making a pest of himself as the barber tried to trim his hair. They were all about 13 or 14.

"Oh, I can't stand it. My beautiful hair," the one in the chair groaned. Then, in the mirror, he gave his pals a grin. They giggled, then laughed out loud.

The barber stood back from him. "Do you want your hair cut or don't you?"

The boy settled down and was quiet. The other two snickered.

The barber swung around to them. "And you two either behave yourselves or get out of here."

They settled down too and pretended to read some tattered magazines. It was then the barber glanced towards the door and saw Jeanie.

"Something I can do for you, young lady?" he asked.

The boys began to whistle. The barber shot them a look

and they stopped.

"I'm looking for—for . . ." she stopped.

"Who?"

"I'm looking for Melvin Hobbs," she said. "Do you—do you know him?" She took a chance on coupling the name the tall woman mentioned with her own last name.

"Mel? Oh, sure." The barber looked up at the big round wall clock. "He's at the tavern by now. He's there nearly all the time. End of the block, Blue Star Tavern." He waved his hand in a northerly direction.

She nodded, "Thank you." But a sinking feeling took hold of her. Usually in a tavern? At this time of day? Well, maybe he was on vacation so he could go to a tavern any time he pleased. At least he wasn't in jail. She was thankful for that, in case he really was her father.

Chapter VII

Jeanie had her doubts about going into a tavern. What would Mr. and Mrs. Taylor say when they heard? And Mrs. Keyes at the Home would have a perfect fit. She could almost hear her saying, "What got into you? You should know a tavern is no place for a young girl." Yes, she knew, but she couldn't let that stop her. She had to find out about Melvin Hobbs.

She smoothed back her hair and looked down at her clothes. Would he like her better if she had worn her pink striped dress and scarf and sandals? Or wouldn't it make any difference that she was all sweaty in a wrinkled blouse and shorts and dusty sneakers? Well, she'd have to wait and see.

She walked north past some more run-down shops and stood, shortly, in front of the Blue Star. A sour, fermented smell came out through the open door. Enough to make you puke, she thought. How could anyone stand it? Well, she guessed, you get used to it if you visit a tavern often.

She hated to go into the dimly lit place, but she'd look dumb standing outside a tavern—as though she were craving a drink or something. Finally she took a deep breath—she almost gagged on the stale odor—braced her shoulders, and stepped inside. It was like going into a movie house in the afternoon. She remembered how stupid she felt one day when she stumbled down the aisle and fell flat on her face. Everybody went "Shh-h." She all but crawled into the nearest seat.

She didn't want to do something like that now. So she stood in the gloom for a moment until her eyes grew used to it. Then she saw the bar along one side. Several men stood in front of it, drinking silently and watching a rerun on a television set high up in a corner. There were a few little tables too. But only one was occupied. A man sat at it with his head bent over a half-empty glass.

The whole place was warm and stuffy, and the perspiration on her neck began to itch. But, she guessed, that was as much from nervousness as from the heat. An electric fan stood on a stand in one corner, stirring the stale air. She couldn't help wishing it were an air-conditioner instead.

Since she had never been in a tavern before, she decided the bartender would be the one to speak to. As she went towards him, one of the men looked around.

"Oh, ho ho! Look at this," he said in a gravelly voice.

Jeanie almost turned and bolted out the door. But she had to find out if one of these men were her father.

The bartender stopped wiping, slung the frayed cloth across his shoulder, and put his hands on the bar. Leaning forward, he looked at her. "This is off-limits to you, Sis," he said. "Are you looking for someone?"

"Yes. Is—is Mr. Hobbs here? Melvin Hobbs?"

"Right over there," the bartender waved towards the man at the table.

"Oh, ho ho!" the gravelly voiced fellow said again and laughed. "She called him *Mr.* Hey, Mel, here's a chick for you. A polite chick."

The man at the table raised his head as she went towards him. With the afternoon light from the doorway falling on him, she could see he was a thin man with stiff, mouse-colored hair like hers. And he wasn't very old. He must have been pretty young when she was born.

She tried to rehearse what she should say to him, but she couldn't collect her thoughts. She went up closer to the table, wishing he would say something. He just stared at her in silence. Oh please, she begged inwardly, please let everything turn out all right. What was she doing? Praying? How could she pray when she said she didn't believe in God? Oh, she was all mixed up.

Finally, in an almost squeaky voice, she asked, "Are you Melvin Hobbs?"

"Yeah, what do you want?" He sounded rougher than she had expected.

"I'm—I'm Jeanie Hobbs."

He straightened a little. "Jeanie Hobbs?"

"Yes. Are you my father?" That was more blunt than she had intended.

He opened his mouth but said nothing. The silence pounded in her ears. He squinted up at her, then opened his eyes wide. They were yellow like hers.

"Well . . ." he hesitated. "How should I know?" he said at last and leaned over his glass as before.

She didn't know what to say, so she just stood there twisting the handle of her handbag. Then, after a long moment, he looked up again and seemed surprised to find her still standing there. He motioned to a chair.

"Here, sit down. Let me look at you."

She slid into the chair and waited.

"Do you have any money?" he asked.

"A dollar and a few cents." Why would he want to know that, she wondered.

"Well, get yourself a soda." With a limp hand he signalled the bartender. She ordered orange pop.

Melvin drained his glass quickly and said, "Bring me another."

The bartender took enough out of her dollar for both orders. She saw she had just enough left for bus fare back to the Taylors—if she went back. She wondered why Melvin didn't pay the bartender, but then she guessed it was all right to treat your own father.

She found his glance searching her. She looked back. His yellow eyes, and his hair, even the stiff way it stuck out over his forehead, yes, she could easily be this man's daughter. Oh, there would have to be proof—birth certificates and stuff like that—but as far as she was concerned, he was her father. And she had a strong feeling that he felt the same way.

Yet misgivings were coming thick and fast. Did she really want him? Yes, she told herself. She was just nervous. She had hoped for this moment so long and talked about it so much. And maybe he wasn't always like this, drinking in the afternoon. She just couldn't let this chance go.

Melvin began to nod slowly. "Yeah, you could be. You look enough like her."

He must mean her mother. That sounded good. She looked like her mother too. Shifting forward in her chair, she asked, "Does she live with you?"

He wagged his head back and forth vigorously. "No."

So that was the reason Melvin was this way. A gladness came over her. If he had a family, he wouldn't be loafing here in a tavern. Well, she'd have to find her mother later. But right now her father was here in front of her.

Her heart was thumping. "Maybe I could come and live with you . . . like a family."

She hoped he could see how desperately she wanted this deep down inside of her. But he only looked at her as though she had lost her mind.

"No," he snarled. "Now go on, get out of here." He turned his back. "I'm getting along OK alone. I don't want anyone butting into my life."

Shocked, her breath stopped for an instant. She felt as though someone had thrown a bucket of ice water over her. Then she took a deep breath. She had one last chance.

"Where is my mother?"

He twisted his head halfway around. There was a different look in his bleary eyes now. "Dead."

An icy stab shot down through her, and tightness gripped her chest. How could just one word make her feel so absolutely alone? There was an emptiness in her as though her heart had drained all the way down to her feet. Her father didn't want her, and her mother was dead.

Melvin was saying, "She left me five years ago. She died in a train accident a little later. Now go on, get out of here," he repeated with an impatient wave towards the door.

The gravelly voiced fellow must have been listening. Before she could move, he said, "Well, she's a pretty big girl now, Mel. If you don't want her, maybe you could give her to me to wash my dishes and scrub the floor."

Just as though she were an object to be handed around. The words cut and twisted through her like a corer going through an apple and taking out its insides. She turned and faced the man. He chuckled low in his throat, parting his lips just enough to show his broken front teeth. She felt like spitting at him. She looked quickly back to her father.

"Stop yakking like a fool," Melvin said to the man. But there was no anger in his voice, just annoyance. If he loved her

43

as a father, he would have been mad when someone hurt her feelings. He would have protected her. Mr. Taylor, with his round, ruddy face would never have let anyone hurt Sue like that.

She wondered if maybe her mother didn't want her either. And why did neither of them ever visit her at the Home? It wasn't that far away. She thought she could have stood anything if she only knew they had wanted her.

She swallowed hard and kept her eyes wide open so she could hold the tears back. "OK," she said as evenly as she could. "Good-bye."

Then she stumbled out through the door and turned towards the corner where the bus would stop. But no matter how hard she fought to compose herself, her eyes welled up. Was this the feeling grown-ups meant when they said your heart was breaking? She wished she were dead like her mother.

Her last chance was gone now. Maybe she shouldn't have come. She might at least still have her dream. Now she had nothing to hang on to. She would be leaving the Taylors too, in a few days. And where would her life go from there?

Chapter VIII

Jeanie blinked her eyes fast, because it was hard to see. Was she being punished for taking Mrs. Taylor's money or for saying she hated God? But if there were no God, how could He punish her? Oh, her mind was darting in all directions like a flock of sparrows.

Then loud jeering voices broke in on her tormented thoughts. She had come abreast of the barber shop. The straggly looking boys were fooling around in front of it. The one who had a haircut was being jostled playfully by the other two.

"Cool it," he yelled as they tugged at his collar, brushed his shoulders, and otherwise pretended to spruce him up. Then he noticed Jeanie.

"Well, did you see old Mel?" he asked in a taunting voice.

"It's none of your business," she snapped at him. They all crowded around her. She tried to push past them, but the one who had spoken to her caught her arm.

"Hey, hey, don't get so smart." Then he grabbed her purse. "Any money in this?" He swung it out of her reach as she snatched at it.

Then he tossed it to a second boy. Just as that one was opening it, Jeanie got her hands on it. But he tugged it away fast and threw it back to the first boy. As it flew through the air, everything fell out of it. The first one caught it, and the other two bent down quickly to grab up her few possessions.

"That stuff belongs to me," she screeched. "Give it back to me." She pounded on their bent backs.

Oh, this was like a nightmare—one horrible thing after the other. What else could happen to her? If she wasn't being punished, what was the answer?

Then she was conscious of someone coming quickly along the curb on a bike. A tall form jumped off and strode towards them. Next a long arm reached across the two who were crouching down and grabbed the first boy by the shirt-front.

"You give me that purse," he ordered.

Jeanie nearly fell over. She looked up into the long face of Paul Krampf from Harvey Home. He handed her handbag to her while his lumpy fist still clutched the boy's shirt-front. Then he told the other two, "And you put all those things back."

Jeanie held the handbag out to them and into it they jammed the items they had picked up. Then with wide eyes they turned and raced off down the street.

"Now you get out of here," Paul told the first boy, releasing him with a strong shove.

As the boy followed his pals at full speed, Paul shouted after him, "And don't bother this girl anymore, or I'll kick the daylights out of you."

Jeanie was so relieved she wanted to cry. She felt as though she had wanted to cry all her life, but she couldn't now in front of Paul Krampf. So again, she held her eyes wide open without blinking.

"It's OK now," Paul said, patting her shoulder. "They won't come back."

At his kind words Jeanie wanted to cry more than ever. "Thanks—thanks for helping me." She hoped her voice sounded all right.

"Think nothing of it," he answered with a slow smile. He seemed taller than she remembered him at the Home. Then he stood back, folded his arms, and looked at her in a puzzled way. "Jeanie Hobbs, what the heck are you doing in Regents Hill?" Before she could answer, he added, "And where do you live now?"

"I live with the Taylor family near Emmetsville," she told him and was glad the lump in her throat went down when she swallowed. She could talk more evenly now. But she didn't want to tell him why she had come to Regents Hill. Instead she asked, "Where do you live? Aren't you at the Home anymore?"

"No." Paul's eyes took on a faraway look for a moment, but he smiled quickly again. "I'm with the Wilson family right over that hill." He pointed southwest of town. "They're OK."

But Jeanie could recognize the tone in his voice. It had a sound that said, "good enough, but I'd rather be someplace else." She had felt that way often enough to know.

It seemed funny, she thought. At the Home he was always deviling her and she was always snapping at him. Then she'd call him Horseface and he'd walk away and leave her alone. Now it seemed that he was the only one in this whole lousy town who didn't try to hurt her.

"Where are you going now?" he asked.

"Back to the Taylors."

"How? That's pretty far." He caught her arm. "You're not dumb enough to hitchhike, are you? It's not safe. You don't know what kind of creep would pick you up."

His eyes were serious. Strange, but she saw that they were a deep, dark blue. She had never looked at him long enough to find that out before.

She shook her head. "No, I'm taking the bus." Glancing over her shoulder she saw it approaching. "Here it comes now."

He gave her arm a little press before he let go. The lump came back into her throat. He told her hitchhiking wasn't safe as though he cared what happened to her. Not bossy, like a grown-up, but well—like he really cared. Her own father didn't even ask how she got here or how she'd leave. She quickened her steps to the corner.

Paul kept pace with her. "Well, that's good," he said. "I mean about your not taking a lift."

She didn't know what to say except, "Thanks again."

"Think nothing of it." He backed away, making a swift motion like a little wave. Then he jammed his hands into his pockets and walked towards his bike. She watched his awkward, shambling steps for a moment and wondered if anyone cared about him.

The bus door was opening. As soon as she was on, the driver started away. The quick lurch almost threw her against the front seat. Flopping down heavily, she reached into her handbag for her fare. But where was her little change purse? She searched again. Then frantic, she dumped everything onto the seat. Her pencil was there, the folded piece of paper,

her comb and small mirror and handkerchief, but no change purse. It might have landed in the gutter when that creepy kid threw everything up for grabs.

Slowly she put all the items back into the handbag. She had to tell the driver, but he looked so big and grouchy, she hated to approach him. She didn't have to. He was looking at her in the mirror above the windshield.

"Your fare, young lady," he called out over the rumble of the bus. "You didn't pay your fare."

"I—I don't have any money."

"What?"

"I don't have any money. I—I," she stammered. "I lost it."

"Well, you can't ride without paying."

"I could get it for you when I get off." As soon as she said that, she wondered how. Run all the way from the road into the Taylors' house and ask for it? Ask Mrs. Taylor, whom she had stolen it from that morning? But she didn't have to worry about that.

"Sorry," the bus driver said.

"Well, then I'll have to get off." She had never felt so small and inferior in her life. Then she added lamely, "Maybe I can find it"—as though he cared.

He pulled onto the shoulder of the road and opened the door. No sooner did she set foot on the ground than a rumble of thunder sounded. It drowned out the noise of the bus starting up again. Would she be caught in a storm now on top of everything else? She would never want to live through another such day. She wished she could go somewhere and hide. Her throat felt so tight it hurt.

Another rumble of thunder warned her to hurry. Turning back to town, she ran all the way. A short distance from the barber shop she stopped and looked around cautiously. Satisfied that there was no sign of those creepy boys, she took a guess at the spot where her handbag fell and started to search. Nothing was lying anywhere—in the gutter, against the building front, in the doorways. Nowhere. It was gone. One of them must have taken it when they were picking up her things.

What would she do now? Maybe her father was still in the tavern. Could she ask him? No, she told herself. If he didn't want her, she wouldn't go to him for anything. Besides, he was probably broke. Why else would he expect her to pay the bartender? There was only one thing to do—walk back to the Taylors' place. But it was such a long way, she hated to think of it.

She started out. Thunder kept rolling overhead. The day was darkening, and flashes of lightening made her flinch. She was never out in a storm alone before. It was getting scary. She walked faster and faster, but she didn't get very far before the clouds opened. The rain came down in buckets-full. In a couple of minutes she was drenched. Then up ahead she saw a bus shelter—one of those little open-fronted buildings with a bench against the back wall. She ran as fast as the driving rain would let her.

Just as she reached it, she heard a voice, garbled by the storm, calling. She dashed into the shelter and peered out through the veil of rain. Someone was coming from the opposite direction on a bicycle. It was difficult to see, but she guessed it was a man. She looked around to find out to whom he was calling. She saw no one.

Then another shout reached her. "Hey, Jeanie." It was Paul Krampf again.

He skidded to a stop, sending a stream of water up from the front wheel. His dark hair was plastered down over his ears and forehead. And his drenched clothes stuck to his gangly frame, making him look taller than ever.

Leaning his bike against the shelter, he stepped in and wiped the rivulets from his thin face. Then, slowly, he grinned at her. "You're the darndest person to catch up with."

"What do you mean, and what are you doing here?"

"I was trying to catch up with the bus you took. How come you're back here?"

Jeanie wondered if they were both going crazy. "Why did you want to catch up with the bus?"

He grinned again while he reached up to squeeze the water out of his hair. He was making her mad, and for a split second she felt like calling him Horseface. But she didn't. Thoughts of what happened to her in town flooded back. He was the only one who treated her like a friend since she came to Regents Hill.

Chapter IX

Paul sat down on the bench and explained. "After you caught the bus, I was riding back towards the lumber yard where Mr. Wilson works. I had a message for him from his wife. That's why I was in town instead of weeding a potato patch." He stopped to chuckle lightly. "Then I spotted this lying on the sidewalk." In his hand was her little yellow change purse. "I saw your name scratched inside."

"I know," she said, feeling a little silly. "I put my name in everything I own."

"But it was empty," Paul added quickly.

"I could have guessed that. Those creeps must have stolen it." She hoped he didn't think that she would accuse him of taking it.

"Well," he went on, "I told Mr. Wilson I better try to catch the bus and give it back to you. But why did you get off the bus?"

"My fare was in this." She held up her change purse. "So I got off to look for it. The driver wouldn't let me ride free anyhow."

"If I had any money, I'd give you enough to take the next bus," Paul said. Then he exclaimed, "You were back there in town again while I almost pedaled my legs off to catch you?"

"I guess so." Jeanie was puzzled. "But how come you got past me?" Again she wondered if they were both going crazy.

For a moment Paul's face looked as though he were the victim of a joke. Then he brightened. "Oh, I know. I took the shortcut over that way a couple of blocks." He flung his arm out in a wide arc. "It cuts off that broad curve in the highway that the bus takes. I'll bet you got off there."

She nodded.

"I nearly caught it once," he added. "But then the rain started and I couldn't keep up."

He took off his shirt to wring the water out of it. She could see his ribs outlined on his skinny side and wondered if he got enough to eat.

He missed the meaning of her look and said, "Oh, I'm sorry. I guess it's bad manners to pull my shirt off like that." He struggled back into it.

"Oh, that's OK," she said and stared out into the rain. The lonely, low, empty feeling was filling her again.

Paul buttoned his shirt halfway up and ran his hands over his wet hair. "You never said why you came to Regents Hill in the first place," he told her.

"I came to find my father."

"Did you find him?"

"Yes, I found him." She went back to the bench and sat down.

Paul turned and looked at her. He smiled widely and wagged his head from side to side. "You did! By gosh, you sure are something else, Jeanie." He slapped his knee. "You always said you'd find your parents. I honest-to-goodness thought you were fooling."

He sounded as though he were cheering her for winning some kind of race. Then his smile faded. "Well, why aren't you happy?" he asked. "Aren't you going to live with him?"

"No—he doesn't want me." She couldn't go any further. All the tears she had kept back for so long gushed forth and she sat there and sobbed until her head ached, her eyes burned, and her throat felt sore. Finally, she quieted. She felt relieved in a way and yet wished somehow she hadn't let go like that. She always tried not to let anyone know how she felt deep down.

Paul was twisting his hands uncomfortably in his lap.

She glanced his way and said, "I guess I'm just a big crybaby."

"No. No, you're not. I'm awfully sorry, Jeanie. Honest I am. I shouldn't have asked you about him."

She dried her eyes and told him everything. "And that's the whole lousy story," she ended, and began to cry softly again. "I thought real parents loved their kids."

Paul patted her shoulder briefly. "Don't cry, Jeanie." He

went back to twisting his hands. "They say the ones you go through hard times with are the ones you love the most." He paused for a second. "Your father was never near you enough to go through anything with you."

She sniffled. "But he never even told that guy off who insulted me."

"Oh, your father probably didn't mean for you to be hurt. Don't let it worry you. Maybe he felt you'd be worse off with him and he wanted to drive you away."

"Well, he sure did that." The thought made her cry again.

"Sh-h," Paul soothed. "Don't, Jeanie. Someday you'll be all grown up and you can make a home of your own. That's what I keep telling myself."

She wiped her tears away and looked at him. There was great tenderness in his eyes. He reached around her shoulder clumsily and pressed her close for a moment. Then he withdrew his arm quickly and stood up to look out at the rain. But his gesture gave Jeanie more comfort than she had ever felt in her life. And he had patted her shoulder too. She remembered how she had envied Sue that affectionate touch. She went to stand beside him.

"Hey," he said, "it's stopping. The storm's almost over."

"It's about time." She tried to smile, but the world still looked bleak and gloomy.

Just then a monarch butterfly flew from the lee side of the bus shelter. It fluttered a little and settled on a blade of wet grass, swaying to and fro. Its orange, brown, and yellow sections were outlined in black. If little Molly were here, she'd be after it in a flash.

"Look," she said to Paul, "its wings are like stained glass."

"Yeah," Paul agreed. Then he turned and looked at her. "You know, you ought to be a poet. You have nice thoughts."

"Gee." Jeanie was flustered. Then she grew bitter again. "But what good will it do me? I like to paint too, but . . ."

"Aw, don't say that. Take a liberal arts course if you go to college—or night school."

"Liberal arts?"

"Yeah, poetry, writing, painting, making statues, stuff like that." Paul sure surprised her. Where did he hear such things? He went on, "I had an aunt who took that in college."

"You did? Well, if you had an aunt like that, how come you

were in that crummy Harvey Home?"

Paul looked across the highway over the open fields beyond. "My mother died, and my father kept my two sisters and me for a while. Then he ran away." Paul shifted his weight from one foot to the other. "My grandmother took my sisters, but she couldn't take me. And I guess nobody else wanted me."

It sounded like her own story. Was it that way with most of the kids at the Home? Life sure was rotten. You try to correct it, and what does it get you? Just more heartaches like she got today. You might just as well not expect anything to change or get better.

"I guess we're in the same boat," she said.

Paul didn't answer for a moment. Then he said, "Yeah, but you just got to forget about it." He shifted his weight again. "When I was little, I used to gripe over and over when something went wrong. My father always told me, 'Never fight a battle more than once.' So . . ."

That made sense, she thought, but it was hard to forget when you hurt so much.

Then Paul tossed his head and grinned down at her. Reaching out to the side of the shelter, he pulled his bicycle to him. Then he held it steady.

"Jeanine Hobbs, get aboard. I'll drive you home." There was a chuckle in his high-tone words.

"You used my full name," she said, surprised.

With a sheepish look he nodded. "Yeah, I sort of like it." Then he laughed. "Remember Mrs. Selby? She didn't believe in nicknames. She always called you Jeanine. Yeah, I like it."

She slanted her eyes at him. "You mean it doesn't sound like a pair of pants?"

"Aw, I was only joking that time."

"That's OK, and Paul . . ."

"Yeah?"

"I'm sorry I called you Horseface."

"Yeah," he repeated. Then he grinned and motioned to the rear of the bicycle. "Well, get on in back." He straddled the seat and waited for her.

She didn't move. Paul was proving a better friend than she ever thought she'd have. Now she was wondering about after today. Paul was around 14. Would he stay with the Wilsons until he was 16 and then be on his own? If that was the way things turned out, she'd probably never see him again.

"Paul, I'm glad we're friends."

"Same here. Now get on. We have pretty far to go."

"That's just it. It's too far," she said. "You might get into trouble for taking so long to get back to your place."

"Think nothing of it." That seemed to be his pet saying. "I can take you most of the way anyhow."

Settling herself on the rack over the back wheel, she wondered what she would hold onto. Maybe she could grab the belt of his pants. But that would look fresh.

"Well, hang on," Paul called over his shoulder and started out.

Quickly she reached for the back end of the long banana-shaped seat. Ah, that was good, she could steady herself easily with that.

The rain had stopped completely now, and Paul pedaled steadily. They didn't speak because the wind would swoosh away any words they might say. Jeanie began to think of what would happen when she reached the Taylors. It seemed so long since she left there—more like three days instead of only part of one. She was trying to form excuses and apologies in her mind when a loud sound cut in on her thoughts. They were at another bend in the highway.

"Sounds like an accident," Paul shouted back to her.

"Where?" she yelled.

"Up past the turn there."

They were curving around a high cutbank that hid everything from view. But the horn of whatever was hit blared continuously. When they had almost completed the curve, they saw the steaming hulk of a black car across the highway. Its grill was smashed in and wrapped around the end of the guardrail. The driver was hanging halfway out the door, with his head bleeding onto the shoulder of the highway.

Paul braked the bicycle. They both jumped off and ran across to the wreck. When they reached the driver, Paul bent over him. But something held Jeanie back. *Oh, it couldn't be . . . it mustn't be!* Then Paul pulled out his big wrinkled handkerchief and carefully wiped the blood from the man's face. She could see now. There was no mistake about it. She thrust her closed hand to her mouth and bit cruelly into her knuckles. The man was Mr. Taylor.

Chapter X

Paul felt in under the steering wheel and around Mr. Taylor's legs. "He's pinned in tight." He glanced around as though searching for something. "We ought to prop his head up a little."

When Jeanie didn't move, he looked up at her. "Gosh, Jeanie, what's wrong? Your face is all white."

Shakily she tried to point. "That—that's Mr. Taylor."

"Mr. who?"

"Mr. Taylor. It's his family I live with."

"Oh, goodgosh!" He looked in both directions along the highway. "I wish someone would come along." He kept mopping the blood oozing down Mr. Taylor's face. "Drag the bike over here. Maybe we can prop *it* under his head."

"Is he—is he . . ." She was afraid to ask it, but she had to know. "Is he dead?"

"Not yet. Now get the bike."

Mechanically, she brought the bicycle from the other side of the highway. Paul slanted it against the battered car. Then stripping off his shirt, he handed it to Jeanie. She crumpled it into a ball, and they cushioned it beneath Mr. Taylor's head.

Then kneeling, she took Paul's handkerchief and sponged off the gray face. Suddenly, the shuddering noise of a truck stopping caught her attention.

"What happened, kids?" a hoarse voice called.

"We don't know," Paul answered. "It happened before we got here."

Jeanie ran towards the truck. "We need a doctor quick," she yelled up to the driver. It was hard to be heard above that horn.

The driver grabbed up his CB radio mike and spoke into it. "Break one-nine." Someone answered. Then he said, "Break nine. This is Moby Dick. I have a ten-eighteen. Car accident, Route 34, east of Regents Hill near the 15th marker. Will need a ten-thirty-two." Someone spoke on the other end again. Then the driver, looking towards the wrecked car, said, "I only can see one fellow. He looks pretty bad."

He must mean Mr. Taylor, Jeanie thought. She knew his other words were CB talk, but she couldn't understand it. "Call a doctor and an ambulance," she told him.

"Just did," he said as he lumbered down from the high seat.

He pried up the hood of the car and disconnected or cut the wire to the horn. It was good to have the blaring stopped. Just then a car pulled up, then another and another. Everyone was asking questions that she and Paul couldn't answer. She wished they would leave instead of gaping at Mr. Taylor. She kept watching his gray face, hoping he would open his eyes, but he didn't. Sometimes a slight bubble would form as the blood crossed his lips. He was still breathing. That was something to be thankful for.

Then a clanging, screeching sound reached her ears. An ambulance and police car sped down the highway towards them.

When an officer asked, "Do you know his folks?" Jeanie gave them all the information she could. Finally, after nearly an hour, Mr. Taylor was lifted gingerly from the wreckage.

As he was put in the ambulance, Jeanie begged, "Please, can I ride to the hospital with him?"

"Sure." The hospital attendant helped her into the ambulance. Just before he shut the door, she saw Paul out of the corner of her eye. He straddled his bike, looked back at her briefly, and waved. Then he pedaled off in the direction from which they had come, with his soiled, wet shirt hanging loosely on his shoulders.

Inside the ambulance, she knelt beside the stretcher. As they started out, the wail of the siren cut through her. She wished she could turn it off. Then she leaned close to Mr. Taylor's face. "Mr. Taylor, do you hear me? Mr. Taylor, please open your eyes."

The attendant said, "He doesn't hear you. He's unconscious."

"Oh," she said, and just knelt there. Her thoughts darted from one thing to another. What if Mr. Taylor would die? Oh, she didn't want to think of that. Of all the men of the families she had lived with, he was the nicest. He was kind to her. He wasn't like Mr. Strunk, who treated her like a relative he didn't want around. Nor like Mr. Bartley, who acted as though she were a servant just there to work for him. And certainly not like her father, who didn't want her at all. No, Mr. Taylor treated her well and now, maybe, he was dying.

She knew she hurt him and Mrs. Taylor when she decided to provoke them into sending her back to Harvey Home. She'd eventually be sent to another foster family, but she'd never find a better one than the Taylors. And there was no reason now to keep going from one foster family to another. There was no reason to keep herself from growing to like them or letting them like her. Her hunt was over. She had no hope now of living with her real folks.

"Dear God," she prayed silently, "please make him better." Shocked, she stared at the wall of the ambulance. She was praying to God. Well, so what? She wanted to. But would God hear her? Would He answer her? She guessed she didn't deserve it. Yet she deliberately began again, "Please, God, make him better." Leaning forward, she covered her face with her hands. "I didn't mean it, God," she murmured. "I don't hate You. I only said that to be bad." She was sobbing now. "I don't hate You, God. I didn't mean it. Please let him be all right."

Then she tried to put her arms around Mr. Taylor's silent form. She felt the pressure of the attendant's hands on her shoulders.

"Don't disturb him, please," he said, and then he reached over and stroked Mr. Taylor's forehead, smoothing his hair back.

"Oh, may I do that?" Jeanie asked. The attendant nodded. How many times her hand moved soothingly across Mr. Taylor's cold forehead, she didn't know. But once he stirred and his eyelids fluttered. He didn't open his eyes, though. So she kept stroking and praying.

A short time later the ambulance drew up in front of the Emergency door of the General Hospital in Emmetsville. Inside they quickly wheeled Mr. Taylor away to an examining room, and she was left to sit on a cushioned bench along the corridor wall. Everything was white and antiseptic and cold. She never felt more alone in her life. She wished Paul were there.

Over and over she told God, silently, that she did believe in Him. "Please let Mr. Taylor get better. I don't hate You, God. I never really did."

Several times doctors and nurses came hurriedly down the corridor. She stood up quickly each time. "Is he all right?"

But they always said the same thing, "Don't worry. He's getting the best of care," smiled and went on by.

Finally, she could sit still no longer. She began to walk up and down, twisting her hands in the handle of her handbag. Why didn't they hurry up with their examination? Why didn't they tell her something? She wanted someone to come out and say it was over, everything went well, he would be better soon. She wanted that so badly, she scarcely looked in the direction of the big entrance door when it opened.

Then she was aware of two familiar figures coming towards her.

Chapter XI

The figures were Mrs. Taylor and Sue. Jeanie stood stark still. After the way she left this morning, what could she say to them? But Mrs. Taylor, as she came nearer, held out her arms. Without knowing why, Jeanie flung herself into them and tightened her own about Mrs. Taylor. Sue reached out her thin arms and tried to embrace both of them.

When they moved apart, Mrs. Taylor asked, "Where did you come from, Jeanie?"

Sniffling and stuttering, she tried to speak. At last she gulped hard and said, "I was coming back with Paul—he's a boy from Harvey Home—when we heard the crash. When we got there, I saw it was Mr. Taylor. I rode in the ambulance with him."

Then for the first time a certain thought struck her. "What was he doing out that way?"

Mrs. Taylor took a deep breath. "When he came in from work," she said, "I told him we hadn't seen you since noon. He had a feeling you went to Regents Hill to see that man Melvin. Is that where you went?"

Jeanie nodded and hung her head. "I took the bus fare out of the corn box. But I'll pay it back," she added anxiously.

"I know you will," Mrs. Taylor said softly and went on. "Mr. Taylor had asked around at work today about Melvin. One of the fellows knew him a long time ago. It seems he was out of the state for several years. But the way this fellow talked, Mr. Taylor felt you would be hurt—especially when he checked up and found Melvin was back in Regents Hill again." Mrs. Taylor cleared her throat. "Since there was a storm coming up and it was getting late . . ."

"Dad went looking for you," Sue put in quickly. Jeanie

looked at her, but Sue's face showed no hard feelings nor bitterness.

Mr. Taylor went looking for her! Her own father didn't care what happened to her, but Mr. Taylor worried about her. You have to care about somebody to worry about them.

"Oh, then it's my fault that he had the accident. It's my fault, it's my fault!" She sank down on the bench and pounded her fists on her knees. All she could think of was that if Mr. Taylor died, she'd be to blame.

Then she felt Mrs. Taylor's arms around her again and she was conscious of Mrs. Taylor patting her shoulder. How often she had envied Sue that little sign of affection. How good it felt.

"No, no," Mrs. Taylor was saying. "It's not your fault. You couldn't have known that a storm would come up and that he would go looking for you. The police said he lost control of the car on the slippery curve."

Just then a nurse came towards them. As before, she was going on by, but Mrs. Taylor told her who she was.

"Oh yes, Mrs. Taylor," the nurse said. "You're not to worry. He's getting the best of care." She hurried on down the corridor.

"That's all they would tell me," Jeanie said.

Mrs. Taylor looked worried. "We just have to wait and see." Then she continued, "I thought the police got our name and address from his driver's license. I didn't know you were there with him, Jeanie. I can't tell you how glad I am that you were, and that you rode in the ambulance with him." She patted Jeanie's shoulder again.

Maybe it was the comfort of that caress, Jeanie thought, but she couldn't help herself. She began to pour her heart out. She told Mrs. Taylor everything that happened that whole miserable day. Today sure made a different person of her. She never would volunteer information to anyone before—except to Paul that afternoon. It was none of their business, she felt, and she always stuck to that.

"And now," she finished at last, "I don't have anything to look forward to." She was making an effort not to cry again.

"Oh, sh-h, don't say that. You have your whole life ahead of you," Mrs. Taylor told her. "But I *do* know how you feel."

"No," Jeanie said stoutly. "No, you don't." How could anyone who wasn't unwanted know how she felt?

"Yes. Yes, I do," Mrs. Taylor maintained. "You feel rejected and frustrated. When I was young, I didn't get along too well with my parents. My father was strict. He scarcely spoke to me except to scold or shout. He didn't want me to go around with a certain friend. He had good reason—she came to a bad end—but I couldn't see that." She inhaled deeply. "Maybe if he had sat down and spoken to me about it, I could have understood. So I disobeyed him time after time by going places with her. And I couldn't talk to my mother either. She was a doormat for my father. She never stuck up for herself. Now I know she was to be pitied." Mrs. Taylor's face became very clouded.

"Then one day my father said if I couldn't do as he said, he wasn't my father any longer and that I should get out of the house. We had a terrible fight and I left home. I was 16, and I went to live with my grandmother in another town. I got a job there, and I didn't go home for a long, long time."

So that's what Mrs. Taylor meant when she told Sue to be patient and that she understood Jeanie's problem.

"What happened to your girl friend?" Sue asked.

"She began to drink heavily night after night. About a year after I left home, I heard she had taken her life."

"Oh," Sue said. A sad look came into her eyes, and she rose to walk down to the window at the end of the corridor.

Silence hung like a heavy blanket for a moment. Mrs. Taylor continued, "Then Mr. Taylor and I met and were married. He's a good man, but we didn't have it easy. Never much money. Our first two children died when they were just babies. And we thought we'd lose Sue several times, too. She was never strong. She is still anemic and must watch so that she doesn't drain her strength." Mrs. Taylor looked towards Sue with a sigh. "At school she can't join in things as she'd like to. So she often has been a lonely little girl. That's why we agreed to foster someone from the Home. We thought if Sue had a girl her own age around, someone to keep her company . . . well, it would be good for them both."

"And you got me," Jeanie said. "I'm sorry you didn't get someone nicer but . . ." she had to talk around the lump in her throat. She hated to think of how nasty she had been when Sue tried to be friendly, and how she had picked fights with Sue. "I'll do my best to keep her company any time she wants."

She had always shoved her own problem on others by being hard to get along with. Just because she didn't have her own family, she couldn't be civil to anyone. Mrs. Selby at the Home used to tell her not to make mountains out of molehills. "Try not to expect too much, Jeanie," she'd say in her velvety voice, "and you won't get hurt so deeply."

But, Jeanie told herself, she couldn't help it. When she watched others with their real parents, she envied them so much she vowed she'd find her own. Well, she did and where was she?

Sue came back and sat down with them again.

"I only wanted to point out," Mrs. Taylor was saying, "that having your own parents and family doesn't guarantee anything." She moved close to Sue. "Lean against me, dear. Maybe you can rest." Then she looked towards the Emergency Room door. The strain showed in her eyes. "I do wish they'd hurry. I hope and pray he's all right."

"I prayed for him too," Jeanie said. She didn't look at Mrs. Taylor, but she could almost feel the surprise on her face. "And I'm sorry for what I said about God. I don't hate Him. I only said that to make you send me back to the Home."

"I knew that was why you said it. But, Jeanie, why did you *want* to go back? The Home isn't that much better to live in, is it?" Mrs. Taylor looked puzzled.

"It sure isn't, but well, I didn't want anyone to like me too much, because I was afraid I'd like them too. And then maybe I'd never leave and get to find my real parents."

"Oh, Jeanie," was all Mrs. Taylor said, because just then a nurse came over to her.

"Mrs. Taylor," the nurse said, "we're going to take your husband up for X-rays now."

"But how is he?"

"He's doing fine. From what we can determine, he has a concussion, some broken ribs, and a fracture of his left arm.

"Oh, the poor man!" Mrs. Taylor said.

"Now, don't worry," the nurse told her. "He'll be good as new in no time. You can wait in the lounge on the second floor." She pointed to the elevator door. "We'll let you know when we take him to his room. Then you can speak to Dr. Brainard."

"Oh, fine. Thank you, nurse." Mrs. Taylor looked at Sue. "You look tired, dear. Come along." She led Sue and Jeanie over to the other side of the corridor and pressed the elevator button.

But Jeanie felt that she herself couldn't rest until she saw Mr. Taylor and spoke to him. As soon as they reached the lounge, Sue curled up on one of the sofas and promptly fell fast asleep.

"Well," Mrs. Taylor began with a big sigh, "I guess our prayers were answered."

Yes, Jeanie thought, they were. She remembered all the times she said God wouldn't answer her and help her find her own family. But now, she guessed, He had been trying to spare her the grief of meeting her father and being rejected by him.

Mrs. Taylor was looking out of one of the windows and spoke about the clear sky after the storm. "There'll probably be lots of stars tonight," she said.

Jeanie peered out too. "I like stars. I wonder at all the things they're seeing from up there—happy people, sad people, and hurt people—like here in the hospital."

"Yes," Mrs. Taylor agreed. "There's always lots of sadness to balance the happiness. The bitter with the sweet, as they say."

"It's too bad everybody can't be happy all the time," Jeanie said. She was thinking, this is Thursday. On Monday the caseworker from the agency in Emmetsville would come with the papers for Mrs. Taylor to sign. And then Jeanie would be taken back to the Home. How she wished that she hadn't used that old trick to get away from the Taylors! She didn't want to leave now. She just didn't want to.

Chapter XII

As Jeanie leaned back in a chair, the lonely, low feeling of the afternoon crept over her. She wished she could undo all the time she stayed with the Taylors and live it over again. But that was the worst thing about time—when it was gone, it was gone.

She must have dozed off then. The next thing she knew was a gentle shake on her shoulder and Mrs. Taylor smiling down at her. Outside the window there was only darkness now.

Jeanie rubbed her neck where a crick had settled in it while she slept on the chair. Suddenly she was fully awake. She jumped to her feet.

"How is Mr. Taylor?"

"Doing well," Mrs. Taylor answered. She looked tired. "I saw him for a little while. He's sleeping now."

Jeanie knew by her cheerfulness that she wasn't glossing over any bad news. And Jeanie's own relief made the evening as bright as midday. "That's good. Oh, that's good!" she said. "But I wish I could see him."

"Oh, you will later," Mrs. Taylor told her. "And now we'll wake Sue and have a sandwich in the cafeteria before we go home."

At the mention of food, Jeanie remembered that she hadn't eaten since noon and she was really hungry.

Sue was still sleeping on the sofa. She looked small and easily hurt. When Mrs. Taylor woke her, she asked immediately, "How's Dad, Mother? Is he better? May I see him?"

"Fine, dear. Now come along. You'll see him later. We'll have a sandwich, and then I'll call a cab."

The next day, Friday, sped by. Jeanie and Sue took care of things at the house, and Mrs. Taylor went back to the hospital. She stayed until evening.

On Saturday Jeanie offered to do Sue's chores too, so that Sue could go to visit her father with Mrs. Taylor. And when they came back, she had supper all ready.

"I can't cook much," she laughed. "I made hard-boiled eggs and mixed them with mayonnaise. So there are egg salad sandwiches, sliced tomatoes, and iced tea."

Mrs. Taylor hugged her. "Jeanie, that's wonderful. We're awfully hungry."

"We sure are," Sue added. As they ate, she told Jeanie, "We met Mrs. Grange in town. She's our neighbor over there," she pointed southeast, "and she said her husband would drive us to the Dollar Mart right after supper if we had shopping to do. Then we can go back to see Dad, and he'll pick us up afterwards."

"Are they the ones with the two kids?" Jeanie asked. She knew most of the neighbors only slightly, because she never cared before if she knew them or not.

"Yes, a little boy and a little girl," Sue answered.

Jeanie turned to Mrs. Taylor. "Do you think I could baby-sit for them? I mean maybe I could stay with the kids and Mrs. Grange could go into town with her husband when he takes you."

"Oh." Mrs. Taylor was puzzled. "But I thought you'd like to help Sue pick out some records and go to see Mr. Taylor . . ."

"I know. I would, but first I'd like to earn enough money to pay what—what I took out of the corn box." She hung her head. She didn't want to leave here owing a debt.

"Well, yes, you have to pay it back," Mrs. Taylor said, "but you can do that tomorrow perhaps. I'll talk to Mr. Grange about it. But you come with Sue and me this evening."

At the Dollar Mart, Jeanie missed having Mr. Taylor along. He always pushed the cart and seemed to enjoy seeing them buy things. She and Sue picked out a Country and Western hit record, a selection by the Boom-Booms rock group, a Sousa march, and a Johann Strauss waltz.

"We sure have a variety," Sue laughed. "But Mother said she'd like Rock of Ages and Brahms' Lullaby."

The saleslady told her she didn't have those on hand but would order them.

Jeanie asked, "When will they be here?"

"Oh, a couple of days. We'll get them from one of our other stores." The Dollar Mart was a chain store. She handed Sue a pencil and paper. "Put your name and phone number on this and the titles of the records you want. We'll call you when they come in."

Jeanie turned away. She wouldn't be here after Monday. She walked over to the next counter and fingered the straw place mats and fancy little baskets.

Sue's face wore a pleasant smugness when she joined her. "Mother's waiting. We better hurry to see Dad."

When they reached the hospital, Mr. Taylor was sitting up. He looked tired, but he smiled when he saw them. After he kissed Mrs. Taylor and Sue, he took Jeanie's hand. "Mrs. Taylor told me you rode here with me in the ambulance."

Jeanie nodded.

Mr. Taylor went on. "I woke up briefly on the way, and it was so comforting to feel your hand stroking my forehead."

"Do you really mean that?"

"Yes, I do."

She could only smile. Knowing she had helped someone who had been kind to her made her feel so good.

"But Jeanie," Mr. Taylor said, "if I had known you wanted to go to Regents Hill so bad, I would have driven you there. And I wouldn't have let you go into that tavern, either. And Jeanie . . ."

"Yes?"

"I'm sorry about your father." Then he added, "There are all kinds of reasons why people act as they do. We shouldn't judge. So don't be too hard on him."

She nodded silently. She hoped someday she could forget how her father acted.

On the way home Mrs. Taylor kept her promise. She said to Mr. Grange, "Jeanie would like to earn a little money baby-sitting. Do you think Mrs. Grange could use her tomorrow afternoon?"

Mr. Grange looked thoughtful for a moment. Then he smiled. "Oh, I'm sure she could. She's been wanting to see the new picture in town. I'll talk to her as soon as I get home."

When he let them out at their house, Jeanie said to Mrs. Taylor, "Thanks for asking him."

"Oh, you're quite welcome, Jeanie." Inside she told the

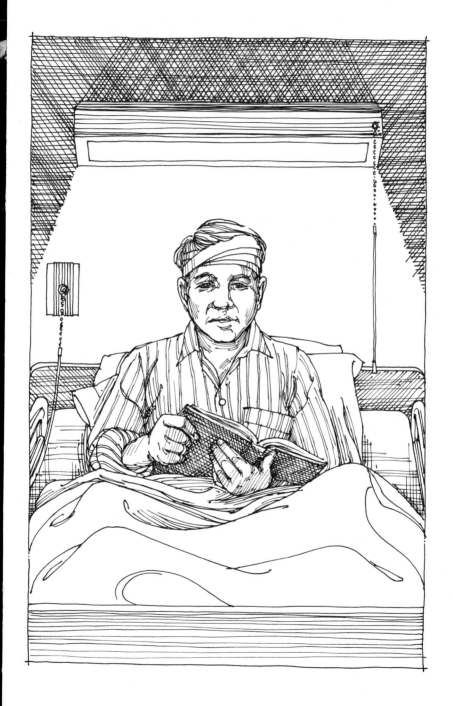

girls, "We better not stay up too late now."

"But we want to hear the records, Mother," Sue said. "Each side just once."

"All right, but we have to get up for church in the morning and . . ."

"Mrs. Taylor," Jeanie put in quickly, "may I go—may I go—to church with you?"

"You certainly may."

Jeanie had only missed two Sundays, but the next morning she felt as if she hadn't gone to church for a year. So much had happened in these last two weeks. It was peaceful sitting there in the polished pew using the dog-eared hymnbook. The sermon had to do with the forgiveness we have when we believe in Jesus as our Savior. The part about forgiveness made her feel much better.

They had Sunday dinner at one o'clock so that Mrs. Taylor and Sue could be at the hospital for visiting hours at two-thirty.

Mrs. Grange called and said, yes, Jeanie could baby-sit for her and that she and her husband would take Mrs. Taylor and Sue in to the hospital and home again. That was fine because no buses ran on Sunday.

So right after she ate, Jeanie walked down the road to the Granges' house.

Little Betsy and Billy were cute, but they kept Jeanie running all afternoon. "Jeanie, look at this," Betsy would say, and no sooner did Jeanie lean over to see what Betsy was pointing to than Billy would call, "Hey, Jeanie, come here quick." Betsy usually wanted to show a picture in a coloring book that she had done, while Billy wanted to call attention to some big, fat bug he had found. He was outside, and Betsy was on the front steps. Back and forth, to and fro, Jeanie went to keep them entertained. Finally, she gave them their supper and cleared the table as the sun was sliding down the western sky.

It would have been much nicer if she could have gone instead to see Mr. Taylor again, but she had to pay her debt. She hoped the shameful feeling about stealing the money would fade away afterwards.

Then she remembered the sermon about forgiveness through Jesus—and the guilty feeling got better.

As soon as the Granges came home, she went back to the

Taylors. She gave Mrs. Taylor the money and watched her put it back into the corn box.

"I'm glad I could return the money before I had to go back to the Home," she said almost to herself.

"Oh, Jeanie," Mrs. Taylor said, "I wish you didn't have to go back."

"Do you really want to?" Sue asked.

"No, I don't want to go back. But I guess I asked for it. I wish I hadn't." At least she felt she wasn't blaming anyone else for it, as she would have done a couple of weeks ago.

"Well," Mrs. Taylor said, "you've grown up these last few days, Jeanie. Being willing to take the consequences of what you did proves that."

Maybe so, Jeanie thought, but she wished it were otherwise.

The next morning was soft and pleasant. The fragrance of flowers came through the doorway, and a blue jay scolded at a squirrel in the elm tree. Jeanie did her chores and helped Sue with hers. The caseworker was expected to come for her after the noon hour. Jeanie could hardly swallow her lunch. After a few bites she gave up.

"I'll get my things ready," she said. There was a tremble in her voice, and she hoped Mrs. Taylor and Sue didn't notice. She hurried with the packing because she couldn't bear to look around at her little room too long. When she went downstairs with her few belongings, she told Mrs. Taylor, "You and Sue go on to the hospital. There's no need to wait. I'll just be going back with the caseworker. You can sign the papers and send them in the mail."

"You're sure you won't mind if we leave? The bus will be here in 10 minutes."

"No, just go ahead," she said, but there was a tightness in her chest, and she wished they'd say no, they'd wait with her. But she couldn't expect them to neglect Mr. Taylor for her.

"Good-bye, Jeanie," Sue said softly. "I'll miss you."

"Good-bye, Sue. I'll miss you, too. I wish I would have been better company for you."

As Mrs. Taylor hugged her in silence and patted her shoulder, Jeanie said, "Tell Mr. Taylor I said good-bye and thanks for everything."

Mrs. Taylor nodded and went out.

Jeanie remembered how she always found it hard to say "I'm sorry" or "Thank you." But, she thought now, "Goodbye" is the hardest of all to say.

Chapter XIII

Once Jeanie was alone in the house, she grew nervous. She toyed with the idea of running away before the caseworker got there. But what good would that do? There was no other place she wanted to go. Her search was over, and new places would make no difference. She would be sent to another foster family soon enough. Walking from room to room, she railed at herself for having spoiled everything. If she could only have another chance she . . .

The doorbell rang. It was Mrs. Keyes from Harvey Home—not the caseworker like other times. Jeanie took her into the living room, and they sat down facing each other.

Mrs. Keyes gave Jeanie a long look. "Well, you did it again, Jeanie. You misbehaved yourself right back to the Home." Another searching look. "Do you really want to go back?"

"No, ma'am, I don't." Everybody in the Home had to say ma'am when they spoke to Mrs. Keyes. Jeanie could never bring herself to say it to anyone else. "I'm sorry I acted the way I did," she added.

Mrs. Keyes arched her eyebrows. "Well, if it were possible to stay here, would you want that?"

"Oh yes. Yes, I would." Jeanie shifted forward in her chair.

"Well, Mrs. Taylor called me this morning," Mrs. Keyes went on, "and told me about your trouble in Regents Hill. She said she thought you had changed your mind."

Jeanie was thinking, she must have called when I was out doing the chores. Then she heard Mrs. Keyes saying, "And Mrs. Taylor asked me if it were possible to let you stay here.

I'm sure it would be, since no papers were signed to the contrary, but I must be certain that you really *want* to stay. And that you won't be up to your old tricks."

"Oh no, I won't," Jeanie assured her. "I do want to stay."

"You know," Mrs. Keyes continued, "I think there'd be a good chance the Taylors would want to adopt you. Or are you still dead set against adoption?"

"No, not any more. Not if it would be the Taylors."

Mrs. Keyes nodded approvingly. "That's fine, Jeanie. Well then, I'll be going. You behave yourself, now. The Taylors are a good Christian family. I'll be in touch with them."

Jeanie almost had to smile at the advice she had heard so often before.

At the door Mrs. Keyes turned to her. "I'm sorry, Jeanie, about your father."

"Thank you, ma'am. I guess I brought it on myself."

"Well, I hope I won't be seeing you at the Home anymore." Mrs. Keyes sounded a little sad as she said that. "Take care of yourself."

"I will, and tell Mrs. Selby—tell her I learned to say 'Thank you' and 'I'm sorry' and tell little Molly—tell her I saw a monarch butterfly." She stopped. She guessed she was talking too much.

Mrs. Keyes nodded and smiled. "Good-bye, Jeanie." She went down the walk.

Jeanie watched until her car pulled out. Just as she was going back into the house, the phone rang. She jumped. What if it were bad news about Mr. Taylor? She hated to answer it. It jangled again.

She picked up the receiver. "Hello."

"Jeanie?" It was a deep voice.

"Yes."

"This is Paul—Paul Krampf."

"Oh." Jeanie let her shoulders slump in relief. "How are you?"

"Fine. I thought I'd just call and see how everything turned out for you."

"Oh, everything's OK."

Paul cleared his throat. "How is Mr. Taylor?"

"He's fine too. He was hurt pretty bad, but he's getting better."

"Well," Paul said, "I just wanted to find out. I found the

Taylors' name in the phone book."

"Yes, it's in the book." That was a dumb thing for her to say. *He* had just said that. Then the happy feeling swept over her again. She couldn't keep it to herself. "Paul," she began. "Paul, maybe I'll be adopted."

"You? Adopted? You always said . . ."

"This is different. And Paul, thanks again, so much."

"Think nothing of it. Good-bye now."

"'Bye and good luck, Paul, in everything."

Putting down the receiver, she smiled. She wondered if she could stand any more nice things happening to her today. Yes, there was one more happy thing she had to do. She took her little suitcase back upstairs and put her few belongings in their rightful places—her underclothes and handkerchiefs in the dresser drawers, her blouses on hangers, her three books on the desk. She tossed her handbag on the desk too.

That evening, when she told Mrs. Taylor and Sue everything that Mrs. Keyes had said, they all joined hands and danced in a circle like kindergarten kids.

"When I called her this morning," Mrs. Taylor said, "she said she couldn't be sure of anything until she came out and spoke to you. I hoped she'd do things this way. I'm so glad she did."

"And Dad is coming home tomorrow," Sue said with a delighted little squeal.

Jeanie sobered. "Do you think he would want to adopt me?"

"Oh sure," Mrs. Taylor said. "We talked about it."

The next day was another soft, warm day with cottony white clouds scudding across a lovely blue sky. Mr. Grange said he'd be happy to drive Mr. Taylor home. And a phone call came from the saleslady at the Dollar Mart saying their other records had come in. That was fine, because now they wouldn't have to make a special trip to pick them up.

That evening, as Mrs. Taylor was leaving with Mr. Grange for the hospital, Sue called after her, "Don't forget to stop at the Dollar Mart and get the records."

It was seven o'clock when Mr. Taylor was helped through the front door by Mr. Grange. He looked haggard and tired, and his left arm was in a sling.

Mr. Grange left immediately, saying he didn't want to intrude on a family reunion. Jeanie served the soda pop, pretzels, and cookies, while Sue played all the records they got on Saturday so that her Dad could hear them. Then Sue opened the package of the ones that were ordered. To all of them the arrangements of Brahms' Lullaby and Rock of Ages were soothing and lovely.

"And here's one more," Sue said. "I think it's for you, Jeanie."

Jeanie sat motionless for a moment. Then she reached for it. The label read "Jeanine, I Dream of Lilac Time." She hugged the record tight against herself before putting it on the turntable. As it played, her eyes stung a little. Did her own mother really like it, and was that why she named her Jeanine? As long as she had never met her, she could always think that her mother *did* love her and didn't give her away because she wanted to.

When the music ended, she said, "Oh, I love it. Thank you so much." Then she asked Sue, "What if I had gone back to the Home?" She wondered, too, if it was Sue's idea alone to give her the record, or all the Taylors'. Either way, she was too happy to care.

"Oh, I would have sent it to you," Sue answered. "Then you'd remember me every time you played it."

"It's a real nice song, Jeanie," Mr. Taylor said. "Now I must get up to bed. I'm tuckered out." They all leaped to his side. "No, no," he said. "You girls just stay here and enjoy yourselves. Mother and I can manage."

Jeanie waited until she heard them clear the last step upstairs. "Your Dad sounded as if I'm one of the family."

"We want you to be," Sue said simply, and started the record player again.

They stomped around chanting, "One, two, three, four," to the beat of the National Emblem march and fell over laughing when it ended. And with the first slow, measured strains of Strauss' *Blue Danube,* Sue twirled around and ran tiptoe across the room, her arms moving in a flowing motion.

"Oh, I'd love to study ballet," she said. "Wouldn't you?"

"No, I'm too clumsy," Jeanie answered. "But you're real graceful."

Sue flushed at the praise. Jeanie felt sure Sue would have to forget about ballet, though. How could she keep up the strenuous practice every day? Regretfully, Jeanie thought of

all the things she could have enjoyed doing with Sue but had never wanted to try.

Finally they played all the records over once more, with Jeanie's song last so that she could go upstairs with its music in her ears.

Up in her little room she opened the dresser drawer and took a deep sniff of the dried rose petals. Then she sank down on her desk chair and began to write her name as she had done thousands of times before. This was the first time she did so since she went to Regents Hill. Jeanine Melissa Hobbs. She stopped and laid down her pen. Her happy feeling of the evening started to fade as she looked at the name Hobbs. She felt, again, the rejection of her father.

Snatching up her pen, she vigorously scratched out Hobbs and then sat staring at it. But that was being spiteful and childish, she told herself. Her father was part of her. She would always have yellow eyes like his, wouldn't she? Besides, she told herself, he couldn't hurt her anymore. And maybe what happened wasn't all his fault. To stay mad at him forever would only take away from her own happiness. She even began to feel sorry for him and wished him good luck.

Bending over her desk, she wrote Hobbs again. Then she put just a light line through it and wrote Taylor instead. Jeanine Melissa Taylor—it had a nice sound. She leaned back in her chair and looked at her three books and her old suede handbag lying on the desk. Wow! Now she would have to rewrite her name in all her things. She smiled at the thought.

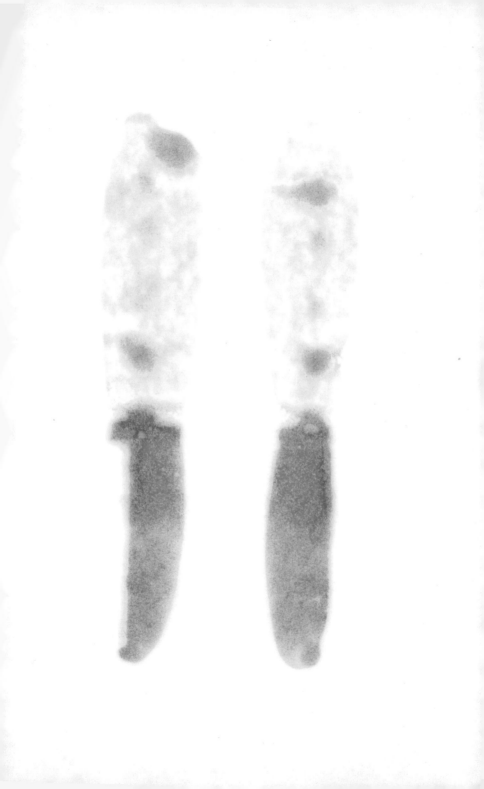

JUV CPH MARKO KATHERIN D.
Marko, Katherine D.
God, when will I ever belong?

Date Due

MAR 2 4 1981			
MAY 0 4 1982			